PRAISE FOR NANCY PICKARD'S
MARRIAGE IS MURDER

"MARRIAGE IS MURDER is a nice mix of caring, wit and sleuthing.''

—*Charleston Evening Post*

"MARRIAGE IS MURDER is bright and breezy, and the problems and patter of the main characters are very much part of today's world. What we have here is another Nick and Nora Charles. . . .''

—*The Hartford Courant*

"Pickard is a bright, lively author with a terrific sense of humor.''

—*Anniston Star*

"Well researched and thought-provoking. . . . probably the best in the Jenny Cain series to date.''

—*Kate's Mystery Books Newsletter*

"The plot is fast-moving, the issues raised thought-provoking. . . . a crackling mystery . . . well worth your time.''

—*The Drood Review*

Books by Nancy Pickard

Bum Steer
Dead Crazy
Generous Death
I.O.U.
Marriage Is Murder
No Body
Say No to Murder

Published by POCKET BOOKS

Most Pocket Books are available at special quantity discounts for bulk purchases for sales promotions, premiums or fund raising. Special books or book excerpts can also be created to fit specific needs.

For details write the office of the Vice President of Special Markets, Pocket Books, 1230 Avenue of the Americas, New York, New York 10020.

NANCY PICKARD

A JENNY CAIN MYSTERY

MARRIAGE IS MURDER

POCKET BOOKS

New York London Toronto Sydney Tokyo Singapore

This book is a work of fiction. Names, characters, places and incidents are either the product of the author's imagination or are used fictitiously. Any resemblance to actual events or locales or persons, living or dead, is entirely coincidental.

POCKET BOOKS, a division of Simon & Schuster Inc.
1230 Avenue of the Americas, New York, NY 10020

ISBN: 0-671-73428-8

First Pocket Books printing October 1988

10 9 8 7 6 5

POCKET and colophon are registered trademarks of Simon & Schuster Inc.

Printed in the U.S.A.

For
Tracy and Andy

Acknowledgments

The author thanks Detective Herb Shuey, Retired Police Officer Robert Clave, Jacqui Bradley, and Karen O'Brien, Service Coordinator, Johnson County Association for Battered Persons. They generously and patiently supplied many of the facts to which I applied my dramatic license. Thanks, as always, to Barbara Bartocci.

MARRIAGE IS MURDER

Prologue

Of course, I wasn't there that night.

Nobody else was, only the two of them, so we'll never know exactly what happened in that small frame house on the corner. But here is how I once imagined it might have been. . . .

Around eight o'clock that Friday night, Eleanor Hanks pulled into the attached garage. She turned off the engine but did not get out of the car immediately to go inside her house.

It was her night out, the one night a month they sent the two older children to visit friends and Dick stayed home with the baby, allowing her to get together with her girlfriends. Tonight, it was going to be at Lizbeth's house, and they would order pizza, and play bridge, and drink diet cola, and laugh their behinds off, free of husbands for a night, free of children, free, real liberated women for a night. "Not that I don't love them dearly," as Lizbeth always said. "I mean, my family are the dearest things in the world to me, you all know they are, but I don't think it hurts to be away from them just a little while now and then, do you? They say it probably makes us better mothers, you know?" Eleanor knew.

But first she wanted to change clothes. She'd spilled barbecue sauce all over her uniform at work. It was an awful stain to get out; she'd never really got the knack of it, so all her uniforms had faint pink splotches, like old bloodstains, that she always prayed the district manager wouldn't notice. Of course, Dick noticed. "You're so messy," he said at least once a day, with the same look of distaste he wore before making love to her, if that's what you'd call it, love. "Why do you have to be so messy, Eleanor? And you're unorganized. You're unorganized and you're messy. The outward appearance is symbolic of the inner woman. You're a mess, Eleanor, inside and out." He thought her brain was messy, too. And "unorganized." She wanted to tell him the more correct word was "disorganized," but Dick wasn't one to be edited by a woman, particularly one with only three years of college to his twenty-two.

Or maybe he really did think her brain was unorganized, totally and chaotically without any discernible organization to it. Maybe he believed her thoughts were popping around up there like corn, wildly, erratically. In the car, Eleanor smiled briefly as she thought: but light, fluffy popcorn evolves from a hard kernel of truth. To which Dick would have said, "You're talking nonsense again, Eleanor. Thought disorganization is a clinically demonstrable symptom of emotional and psychological pathology. You might try now and then to string two coherent, related sentences together, do you think that would be possible?''

She wasn't especially afraid to go into the house. He hadn't been really drunk for some time now. He was sulky, but not outright mean about her Friday nights. And he was pretty good about not hitting her when any of the children were around. God, if he'd hit her very often when they were around, she'd have left him. Wouldn't she have left him? Oh, Lord, she wasn't that stupid, was she? She'd have left him then, wouldn't she? But she'd put in twenty years getting that man through college, was she going to quit now, when he was nearly through that damn thesis, when he was finally going to make them some money and she could finally quit flipping hamburgers? Was she going to leave him now and join the millions of mothers and children in poverty?

Hah. She didn't smile, but only thought the bitter laughter. What did she mean, join them? She was already with them, they could qualify for food stamps or some other government program if he'd agree to it. But, oh, no, not the good professor. A professor's wife, in line for food stamps? An almost-professor's wife. A would-be professor's wife. A failed boy wonder's wife. A fast-food manager's husband. Now, that was funny.

When she heard him pull open the door that led to the garage from the kitchen, Eleanor realized nervously how long she'd been sitting in the front seat of their car. Maybe he wouldn't yell at her, not with the baby in the house.

Dick didn't yell at her.

She watched with trepidation as he walked down the two steps into the garage and then pulled open the door on the passenger's side and leaned in.

''You didn't get my beer,'' he said in his cold, accusing

voice. "I told you to put it on your list, and you forgot, didn't you? You're so unorganized, Eleanor. I tell you to make lists, but you can't even do that. As if you could depend on your feeble brain to remind you of anything! I see you got your frozen cherry cheesecake, which is just exactly what you need on those thighs, but you can't remember a simple thing like my beer. Is it too much to ask that you think of me for once? Can't you think of anybody but yourself? What do you expect me to drink while you booze with those flea-brained friends of yours? Apple juice? Go get me some good beer."

"We don't get drunk," she said quietly in her most careful, neutral voice. "And they're very smart women. And I don't have enough time tonight, Dick. Why can't you get your own beer?" She said it appeasingly, trying to keep the whine, the note of self-pitying complaint that he hated, out of her voice. "You could go get it while I change clothes, and I'll stay with Steven, and you'd be back here by the time I have to go."

"My God, you're selfish."

"Please." She felt desperately tired and gritty, and acutely aware of the fresh stains on her uniform, and she wanted to take a shower and change clothes, and hold the baby for a few minutes, and leave. "It'll only take you fifteen minutes, and I never ask you to do the grocery shopping, I always do it, and I'm just so tired, Dick."

He slammed the door and, absurdly, yelled at her through it, "You think you're the only one who ever gets tired around here, you don't know what tired is! I'm the one with all the stress on me, I've got my thesis to work on and papers to grade and three books to review, and all you do is stand around eating French fries and getting fat at that joint, and I work my fingers to the bone for you, and you can't even do one little thing for me, you're so damn selfish!''

Eleanor stared at him from inside the car, feeling oddly detached from him and from everything happening to her. She thought how easily he fell into clichés in his writing and speaking. He thought he was so original, so brilliant, but nobody'd called him that for the last ten years; he was the boy wonder who turned out to be mostly boy and no wonder. He even looked a little like a cliché standing there, the archetypal perennial student: too tall, too thin, cheeks too smooth, skin too unlined for his age, eyes too fervent and feverish for a forty-year-old man, wearing a pullover sweater and slacks and socks and loafers. Twice a year he read *A Portrait of the Artist as a Young Man,* intoning paragraphs to her proudly, as if it were about him. Once, years before, she'd told him she glimpsed a startling similarity between him and the young James Joyce, but she'd been lying even then, because it was only a similarity of hopes that she had seen. Her hopes. Maybe she was selfish, she didn't know anymore, but she was beginning to think he might be right about that. There was a lot she wanted, maybe selfishly. Was it right to want so much? Was it even realistic? She wanted not to be tired, she wanted not to be afraid, she wanted not to feel pain ever again, she wanted not to have acid in her stomach, she wanted not to eat any more French fries, she wanted her kids not to have to tiptoe around the house when their father was writing, she wanted not to lie to her mother about how everything was all right, she wanted not to be embarrassed that her so-called brilliant husband who had five degrees still hadn't decided what he wanted to be when he grew up, she wanted not to fry another fish sandwich, she wanted not to wash another uniform, she wanted not to pick up any more dirty napkins that people had blown their noses in—she wanted, she wanted, she wanted, she wanted him to get his own damn beer and leave her alone.

"Leave me alone," she mouthed at him. "Get your own damn beer."

"What'd you say?" he shouted at her, and she felt a sudden panic.

Why had she said that? It was the wrong thing to say. Oh, Lord, she knew better than to attack back, she knew the only way to fight him was to go limp like those peace marchers, in mind and body and voice, so he'd finally get frustrated at trying to fight with someone who was no more resistant than a pillow, and he'd slam angrily out of the house, away from her. But dammit, he wasn't going to run out tonight and leave her holding the bag and the baby again. Again! No, not tonight, this was her night, her night, dammit, her one night!

"What'd you say to me?" His voice was louder now, more insistent.

She knew he'd keep after her until she repeated it.

When she didn't answer, he kicked the car, lightly.

Calm down, she commanded herself, but for him as well.

"Tell me." He kicked the car again, harder.

She huddled in the driver's seat, drawing into herself, staring obstinately at the Chevy cross in the center of the steering wheel, trying frantically to retreat to a small, cool, quiet, rational corner in her brain. But she felt the exhaustion, the resentment, bubbling uncontrollably in her like acid, eating its way through her restraints, threatening to spill all over them both—burning, disfiguring, destroying everything. Help me. Help me. Don't fight him, don't fight him, urged the still, quiet, detached voice that sounded as if it were moving away from her down some distant tunnel.

He marched around the front of the car to her side and glared at her through the closed window.

"Tell me what you said, Eleanor!" he demanded furiously, bending down, placing his face close to the glass. Why didn't he just pull open the door? she wondered. Maybe he thought she had it locked, and he was afraid of making a fool of himself by tugging absurdly at it. He hated to look foolish. He was foolish. She hated him.

"Tell me what you said, Eleanor!"

The acid bubbled in her. She clamped a lid on it. A stream seeped through and trickled down her arms, charging them with an overpowering heat and energy that demanded outlet. If he beats me, I'll kill him. I'll kill him. The baby, the baby. I'll call the police. I'll leave him. My babies, my babies. Help me. Help me.

Eleanor tightened her grip on the car keys in her right hand. She could start the car and back out. No, she couldn't do that, because she'd already closed the garage door, so if she did that, she'd drive through the door and then he'd kill her for sure. She heard herself make a whimpering noise, and then she felt her lips move. "And then I won't get to play bridge . . . but look, he has his hand on the door handle, and he's jerking it open, and I can't leave the baby, I can't leave the baby. . . ."

She screamed lightly when he grabbed her upper arm.

"What did you say to me, Eleanor?"

"Get your own damn beer!" she heard herself, to her horror, screaming at him. "Leave me alone, damn you!"

"Get in the house." He grabbed viciously at her hair.

Eleanor screamed at the pain, following it out of the car, stumbling blindly after the pain as he jerked her around the hood of the car, toward the steps, up the two steps, through the door of the house.

* * *

That's how I imagined it after I heard about it.

Oddly, that's nearly as far as it went in my mind. Though I lay in bed, or sat at my desk, or drove my car and replayed the beginning over and over, my mind skidded away from imagining the very end. That, I only visualized in lightning flashes, only heard in snatches. I saw him release the handful of her hair, and I saw her falling to a worn brown carpet. But then the rest of the argument failed to form words in my mind, maybe because I instinctively knew it didn't matter what the real words were that night. Or maybe because touching the pinpoint of the moment of murder is as dangerous as touching the point of a sharpened, swinging sword, as dangerous as entering a dark and holy contaminated place. Sure, I could imagine cursing, pleading, yelling, but only in bursts of sound, as if someone were rolling the dial on a radio. "Damn you!" Static. "Oh, please!" Static. "No!" Static. And then, at some point, at the end of the radio dial, I hear her running into their bedroom, opening the drawer in the table on his side of the bed. I hear a rustle as she withdraws the gun, and I can feel the tremble of her hands. And then he's running—no, walking—into the bedroom, and she says something, and he says something, and maybe he laughs, or maybe he doesn't, and her hands are trembling, and nearly liquid with weakness, and then I feel his moment of dumbfounded, startled precognition. And then there is the sound of a gun going off, and this time it is Dick falling to the worn brown carpet. And at this point in my imagining, I always hear a baby crying.

As I said, that's how I once imagined it.

Now, of course, I know as much as anyone can about how it really happened, how it really ended. Or do these things ever really end? Or do they keep playing themselves out in a thousand strangers' minds, finding places on the pages of the emotional albums of strangers' lives: "Here, this one is a murder I remember, a fellow named Dick Hanks, lived a couple blocks over, boy, I'll never forget that." Not to mention the way a murder lives on in the cycling lives of its children, its intimate friends and implacable enemies.

Now, later, I see it differently, metaphorically. I see them, the two of them, as atomic particles of opposite charge, electron and positron, propelled toward each other at unimaginable speeds until they collided, destroying each other, but in the process creating new and unnamed particles that spun wildly, forcefully, into neighboring lives . . . mine, Geof's, our families, other families.

IT MAY SEEM SUSPICIOUSLY COINCIDENTAL THAT WE—THE police detective I lived with and I, and the new man on the force and his wife—were trading tales of domestic disturbances at the exact moment the beeper sounded, calling the two policemen to the scene of the Hanks homicide. But it wasn't really much of a coincidence. It was just two cops and their ladies, talking about what cops always talk about: cop work, which often boils down to "Domestic Disturbances I Have Known and Survived."

"It's the full moon that does it," Geof said in a joking tone. I knew he didn't believe it, because he had shown me the statistics that proved it wasn't true, no matter what the popular belief about full moons and emergency rooms. "You show me a full moon and I'll show you a town full of men and women beating up on each other. It's lunacy.''

He smiled at his own pun. Obligingly, I groaned.

''The first year I became a cop, and this would be maybe fifteen years ago, I almost bought it on a domestic call, on a full moon, of course. Jenny's heard this story a thousand times.'' He squeezed my hand on top of the table. ''Can you stand it one more time?''

''I love cheap thrills,'' I assured him.

He nodded in mock agreement. ''I know. That's why you live with me.'' With a smile, he admitted the two people across the table from us into the intimate kidding. One of them was Willie J. Henderson, the newest detective on our small municipal force, and the other was his wife, Gail.

Willie was a wiry black man with eight years of a Boston street beat behind him. It showed in the lines that were gouged in his narrow face—giving it the look of African sculpture hacked out of hardwood—and in the prematurely gray hair cropped close to his prematurely balding skull. Geof was the older, taller, and larger of the two men, but compared with Willie, he looked collegiate in his open-necked white oxford shirt, denim trousers, and tweed sport coat. And there I was beside him—blue eyes, blond hair, corduroy pants suit. We looked like a page out of an L.L. Bean catalog. Willie wore black leather jeans, a black leather sleeveless vest, and ankle boots. His wife was dressed in early Montgomery Ward—polyester skirt and sweater, hose, and low black heels. They were handsome together in a life-hardened way, like two uprights in a wrought-iron railing on a widow's walk.

Willie kept his gaze fixed on the scarred wooden table that separated us from him and Gail. He rarely smiled.

She smiled too often, preceding everything she said with a nervous little laugh, a sort of ha-ha, so that you could actually hear the double syllables, like words.

She gave that laugh now. "Ha-ha." And she said, in a high voice that was straining to sound animated, "I'll never forget Willie's first week as a rookie."

Geof waited politely, expectantly. But she only flickered her nervous smile at him, then at me, and returned to sipping her low-calorie beer. Not that she needed to lose weight—she was a little woman, all stark, pointing bones, the sort on whom you want to force spaghetti. During the moment of awkward silence, she began to cough.

"Asthma," she murmured, even managing to smile between coughs. She choked out: "It's why we moved. Ha-ha. No lung power. Willie had to get me out of the pollution. Ha-ha. It was so good of him, leaving the force that way. Willie earned medals, you know. For bravery and marksmanship. Everybody respected him. . . ." The wifely support petered off into another paroxysm of coughing.

"Gail," I said, "do you want to go?"

She shook her head, took a couple of quick drinks of beer, and then a deep breath. The coughing stopped. She placed her hand against her breastbone and pressed it there as if holding an incipient cough in place.

While we waited for her to recover, her husband scanned the clientele. It was a cop's glance: I'd seen Geof level it at parties, at grocery stores, in traffic, even in his own home with his own family—any burglars here? rapists? escaped convicts? He couldn't help it: After years of checking crowds for criminal elements, it was an unconscious mannerism, although it could be disconcerting for the other guests at class reunions and Christmas parties. Having evidently failed to recognize anybody from the FBI's Most Wanted list, Willie returned his gaze to a spot in the tabletop where some previous customer had gouged a deep pit, like a tiny grave in the wood. Now it held his attention as if it contained a corpse.

"I'm all right," Gail insisted weakly.

Geof continued his story: "So I'm cruising along, and I hear a call for officer needs assist on a house burglary." He switched to the present tense and leaned forward, as if he were reliving the moment. "I'm the closest cop to the address, which is 800 Southwest Twentieth Street. I'll never forget that number as long as I live, which I didn't think, at the time, was going to be all that damn long."

"I got a few addresses carved in my brain," Willie said.

"Ha-ha," Gail said.

"It's pitch night." Geof, like most cops, was a natural storyteller. "Clouds over that damned full moon. Foggy as hell. And I come up on a fight, with the other cop in the middle, and he's trying to pull a woman off a man. She's flailing around with one of those fat plastic baseball bats like kids have, and the man's got hold of a toy gun, looks like a sawed-off shotgun. She's screaming, 'He tried to kill me! Arrest him!' Well, the man drops his toy gun. But he grabs the baseball bat and clobbers her between the eyes. She goes down like a demolished building. Thump. On his backswing, he lays the other cop out flat. Thump. 'Stop!' I yell forcefully, as I was taught at the academy." (It was true, I had heard this story many times, but this part, the way he told it, still made me smile.) " 'Lay down your weapon!'

"Well, the sucker lays it down all right, and he picks up the sawed-off shotgun and now I see this isn't any toy.

I figure I'm dead. But damn if he doesn't stare at me for the longest minute I ever lived and then he sprints off into the fog. I can't see him to shoot him. So instead of running after him, I call for a couple of ambulances and tell the dispatcher to send some cars to look for a track star with a shotgun. I figure I'm on my way to a commendation for my amazing display of restraint.'' (That always made me smile, too, and start to laugh in anticipation of the climax. I started laughing now, with Geof nudging me to try to keep me quiet so I wouldn't ruin it for Gail and Willie.) ''About that time, the woman wakes up, and she's frantic. 'Where is he? Where's that son of a bitch!' she's yelling. And I say in my best Canadian Mounties voice, 'We'll get him, ma'am. We'll get that burglar.' '' (Now I'm really giggling, and Gail and Willie are looking from Geof to me, and back again.) ''But she starts beating on me! 'Burglar!' she screams. 'That ain't no burglar, that's my husband, you chickenbrain! You lay a hand on that man and I'll tear your'—excuse me—'fucking legs off!' And she lays into me with the plastic baseball bat, so by the time the ambulances get there, they need three stretchers to haul us all out of there!''

As always, I doubled over as if I'd never heard it before. Gail and Willie seemed amused, if not quite as hysterically as I was. It had occurred to me that maybe Geof told his cop stories again and again just for the pleasure of seeing my reaction to them. As for his language, Gail had obviously been a cop's wife too long to be shocked.

''Ha-ha-ha,'' she said. Willie's narrow face broke into a slow grin, his first of the evening.

''I learned many things that night,'' Geof said ruefully, rubbing the cheekbone that had been broken in that melee. I dried my tears with a cocktail napkin. "Besides the fact that domestic disturbances suck, I mean. I also learned: Don't take anything for granted. Situations are not what they seem to be. People are not who they seem to be. And without Tonto, the Lone Ranger wouldn't have lived long enough to adjust his mask."

He had smiled straight at Willie as he spoke.

"Willie." Gail nudged her husband's arm. "Tell them about Jesse."

"There was this babe on the street once." Willie's voice was as slow and deliberate as his smile. He stared over my shoulder as he spoke. "Clothes all torn up. Cryin'. Standing just inside an alley, like she's hiding. Me and my partner, we pull over and ask her, has she been hurt. She's fair looking, tall like a model, a white gal, lots of makeup, tight silver pants, off-the-shoulder blouse, only it's been *torn* off her shoulder. Gold pointy heels, lots of pretty red hair. Real clean hair. And we're thinking, maybe her pimp did this to her, and we ask her, does she want us to take her to the woman's shelter? She says yes. Gets in the back seat. Still crying, tells us her name is Jesse, tells us her boyfriend beat her up, but she won't give us his name, where they live, nothin' else. All we can do is deliver her. We take her to the shelter. We're standing downstairs, shootin' the shit with the director, and suddenly there's this screaming from all these women upstairs on the second floor. And the director goes running up, and pretty soon she comes back down with our white gal, who is now holding her pretty red hair in her hands. Everything about her story turned out to be true except for one minor detail: Jesse was a man."

"Where'd you take her?" I asked. "Him."

Willie shrugged. "Back to the station. He cleaned himself up. In the men's room." Willie cracked a brief smile, and so did Geof, but I wasn't finding the story very amusing. "He slept in a chair all night."

"What happened to him?"

"Next morning he borrowed some makeup from one of our women officers and made himself gorgeous again. We gave him bus fare and I guess he went on back home to his boyfriend." When he noticed the expression on my face, Willie shrugged again. "There ain't no shelter for some people."

Gail began to cough, at first quietly, as if she were trying to hide it, but it was soon shaking her small body.

"Where's your inhalator?" Willie said.

"Forgot," she choked out. "Home."

He looked annoyed, as if that was a bad habit of hers, but he patted her back perfunctorily.

"Domestic disturbances!" Geof shook his head, and looked ready to wax philosophical on those cases that were the greatest bane and hazard of a cop's existence. But he was interrupted. It was at that moment, which was not really all that much of a coincidence, that his beeper sounded. We all looked at each other with varying degrees of tension and resignation.

Geof sighed. "Is it a full moon tonight?"

When he returned from the phone, he leaned down and murmured, "Reported homicide. Let's go, Willie. We'll take your car."

Then he kissed me quickly on the mouth and said, in what had become a ritual over the two years we'd lived together, "I'm sorry. I love you." I kissed him back and offered my own part of the formula: "Be careful. I love you." There wasn't any need to waste words or time in saying I'd take Gail home, or that he'd wake me up to tell me he was still alive. We knew all that. There had been plenty of shattered days and evenings in which to establish such habits. As always at such times, my consciousness focused on him like a laser, since I never knew if this would be the last time I'd see him. If it was, I wanted to be comforted—later—by knowing we had given our last moment together the respect and attention it deserved.

On the periphery of my awareness I saw Willie kiss Gail.

"I'll be all right." He sounded impatient, angry, eager. He sounded like a cop.

2

GAIL AND I WERE LEFT STARING ACROSS THE TABLE AT each other in a booth that suddenly seemed too large without the men to fill it. Even the air in the room seemed lighter and the lights brighter with the men gone to their appalling jobs.

"Well," I said, one cop's lady to another, "here we go again."

Her hazel eyes were wide and full of fear, but she flickered her nervous smile at me. I smiled back at her. She smiled back at me. I began to feel like one half of two flashing stoplights.

"Do you want another beer, Gail?"

"No, thanks." Her smile flickered on, off.

"Would you like a Coke? Coffee?"

"Uh-uh."

29

"So." I glanced around the room, looking for conversational gambits. When none came to view, I said, "How long have you and Willie been married, Gail?"

She coughed, and her mouth twitched again. "Eleven years."

"He's been a cop eight of those years?"

She nodded, coughed again, smiled again.

The conversation was turning out to be something of a struggle, but I persevered, hoping that if we remained in the bar a while longer, the look of terror in her eyes might fade. I was surprised to see all that fear in her; Geof always told me there wasn't much danger associated with a homicide call unless the killer was still on the premises, which he usually was not. Unless it was a domestic disturbance, of course—they were always dangerous, because they were so full of passion, uncontrolled and unpredictable. And Gail had been a cop's wife a lot longer than I'd been a cop's lover. Maybe I was naive in my security; maybe she was wise in her fear. Was this what I had to look forward to, the fear growing worse the longer I loved him?

"Do you have any children, Gail?"

"Willie, Jr.," she said between coughs. "He's six. And Natalie Renée. She's five. I'm expecting another baby. In June."

This was November, making her three months pregnant, with her husband in a job with less than perfect odds on whether he'd still be alive in six months to kiss the baby. No wonder she looked terrified. Who wouldn't?

There is nothing like one confidence to stimulate another.

"Gail," I said, "it's kind of a secret, but Geof and I are getting married in a couple of weeks." It was, in fact, set for two weeks from that night. We hoped to keep it small, quiet, private.

"Congratulations," she said, and coughed.

"Tell me something—do you ever get used to—"

She didn't even let me finish the sentence. "No. Never."

"Never?"

She shook her head. "It gets worse when you have kids. Then you're scared for them, too." She pushed her half-empty beer glass away. "Would you mind taking me home now, Jenny? I need to let the baby-sitter go. It's hard to find baby-sitters in a new town. I don't want to be late and make her mad at us."

I thought it wasn't really the baby-sitter she seemed scared of losing. After paying the check, I escorted her to my car, a new Honda Accord that was a conservative silver on the outside, a brash cherry-red within. There was a full moon, risen. On the drive to her house, I made another stab at conversation: "Did you have a job in Boston, Gail, outside of your kids?"

"No, but I'll have to now." She was staring out the window when she said it, wistfully. With a visible effort, she returned the polite inquiry. "What about you?"

"Do I have kids? Do I work? No, and yes. I'm the director of the Port Frederick Civic Foundation. To put it simply, we give other people's money away. If you, for instance, were stinking rich . . ."

"Ha-ha," she said.

". . . you might leave your money to the Foundation when you died. Then we would distribute it to worthy causes, like the home for battered women, or we might buy a new X-ray machine for the hospital, or we might sponsor a benefit for handicapped children, or we might help to build a memorial to the Vietnam vets, or we might . . .''

I chattered on, hoping to relax her. And myself. Her fear was beginning to infect me, and I resented it; I felt the symptoms of dry mouth, liquid bowels, rapid pulse, and I didn't want them. She directed me to a neighborhood of nearly identical, run-down rental properties and then to the gravel driveway of one of the small brick houses. The porch light was on. Through the picture window I saw a light, the kind of odd, dead luminescence that only televisions emit. As a child, I had been superstitious about that light, afraid that if I walked through it, it would suck the colors and dimensions from my body, leaving me flat, black-and-white, and trapped like the grinning little people who lived in it. Even as an adult, I couldn't look at a TV glowing in a dark room without feeling briefly desolate.

I put the car in park but left the engine running.

Gail and I stared at her new home.

"I hate this house," she said suddenly, fiercely. I had the feeling it was only tact that kept her from adding, just as fiercely, "I hate this town."

"You miss your old home."

She nodded, and seemed to be holding back tears.

"Well." She took a shuddery breath that turned into a cough; then she flickered her smile at me. "Thanks for bringing me"—the face she turned toward the brick house was bleak—"home, Jenny."

Impulsively, I reached across to touch her arm.

"Things will get better, Gail." I wanted to bolster her morale, but managed only to give her clichés bunched together like a bouquet of plastic flowers. "You've still got Willie and the kids. You'll find a house you like better, you'll make friends. This is a pretty good town to live in, really.''

She grabbed my hand briefly, strongly, but she didn't reply, not even to tell me to mind my own business. I thought I ought to give her a chance to return the favor of passing out advice, so I kept hold of her long enough to say, "Gail, do you have any words of wisdom for a lady who's about to marry a cop?"

"Yes." She opened the door, slid out of the car, and looked back in at me. "Don't." Her smile flickered one last time, and then she pulled her jacket closer around her and trotted off toward her front door. I waited in the driveway until I was sure she was safely inside. For a moment, as she stood on the porch fumbling for her keys in her purse, her small figure was illuminated by the dead light from the TV. She was coughing into her fist when she shut the door.

When I got back to Geof's house—the hideously large and modern one that his second wife, Melissa, had picked out and then abandoned—I climbed to the second floor to take a shower. Then I put on a thick, warm robe and tennis socks. I went down to the kitchen to eat a snack of cream cheese, onions, and salmon on garlic bagels, with a dark Beck's Beer—I may have inherited Swedish skin, but my stomach's Hungarian—while glancing through the newspapers. After a look at the cable network news, I brushed my teeth, spent my usual moment feeling guilty for not flossing, pulled out the alarm on the clock, and crawled into bed—the queen-size one that Melissa Bushfield Vance had picked out and then abandoned for the digital charms of a computer whiz.

"Hello, there," I said to my mental image of her. "Why are you coming to mind tonight, and so cynically?"

It wasn't as if Geof couldn't have said no to the ugly house or the ugly bed. Or the wife. I wished he had. Said no to marrying her, that is. Then maybe I wouldn't get these occasional sinking feelings that I was standing in a line at the edge of a cliff over which two wives had already jumped. Or been pushed by his job? I don't like lines. I'm not crazy about heights. What was I getting into? But how could marriage to him be different from living with him? But if it wasn't any different, why do it?

"Oh, shut up."

By way of punctuating the thought, I switched off the light.

I pulled up the covers and closed my eyes.

They opened again and stared into the chilly darkness of the bedroom. Finally, the nightmare thoughts that I had been holding back crept into my brain, down my spine, into my bowels: Somebody died tonight, somebody else became a killer. It was all my imagination needed to start wondering who, how, why. Something lost and evil was loose in the world again, and nobody would be safe until it was tamed, or caged, or killed. I wasn't afraid for Geof so much as for all the innocent, sleeping people in the world. He, at least, was armed, trained, ready for it. The rest of us were not. By the time I had that thought, every creak of the furnace had become a stealthy footstep and every shadow held a stranger with a knife.

Damn Gail Henderson and her wide eyes full of fear!

I didn't know I had slept until Geof woke me by gently massaging my shoulders. His chin whiskers brushed my earlobe as he kissed my left temple and then murmured the last part of our good-luck formula: "Still here, m'dear."

"Never doubted it." I rolled over gladly into his embrace. Over his bare shoulders I saw the clock: two-thirty. My lips were gummed together with sleep. I licked them before asking, "What happened?"

He was silent for so long I began to fear he had seen something so gruesome he didn't want to tell me about it. Then he sighed. It was a ragged sound dragged up from deep in his abdomen.

"Full moon."

"A domestic disturbance, you mean?"

"To say the least. One dead husband."

"Oh, Lord. It wasn't anybody I know, was it?"

"Dick Hanks?"

"No." I felt relieved, and shamed by it. "Self-defense?"

"I guess."

I kneaded my knuckles strongly into his back, along his spine. He groaned. He was faintly damp and smelled of Safeguard soap. After a night homicide call he always took a shower, brushed his teeth, cleaned and pared his nails. Sometimes he rinsed his eyes, as if he could wash away the bloody sights they'd seen. In the morning, if I looked, I would find his clothes rolled up at the bottom of the dirty-clothes hamper. He was not a fastidious man except when it came to clearing other people's violence from his system before coming to bed with me.

"Do you want to talk about it?"

"Not now. I'm too tired." But then, as if he couldn't stop himself, he said, "He beat her, and she couldn't take it anymore, and she killed him. Shot him. Wham, bam, thank you ma'am. He was forty years old, but one of those perennial students, you know? I don't think he'd ever had a real job, just part-time jobs while he kept piling up the degrees. This time, he was a security guard at the college. Five fucking degrees. What's a man need five degrees for, anyway? Three kids. Two of them were out tonight, but the baby was there. Shit. Two years old. Jesus. The wife's the one who worked, but not at anything that paid worth a damn, just at a barbecue joint. She was supposed to be playing bridge at a girlfriend's house. Eleanor. Dick and Eleanor Hanks. I've called on them before, Jenny. Twice. And there wasn't a damned thing I could do to save either one of them. It's sick. It makes me feel sick.''

I continued kneading his spine until he fell asleep, at which point I could have used somebody to massage my own tense muscles. As it was, I stayed awake a long time, imagining a woman driving her car into a garage. . . .

3

SEVEN-THIRTY, SATURDAY MORNING. ACROSS THE BED-room, Geof was already up and dressed in a white shirt and dark gray trousers. His hair, brown and thick, looked as if he'd combed it with his fingers; I sniffed, inhaled spicy aftershave. He was gorgeously appetizing, but I sensed that my nose was pressed up against a bakery window and I was lusting for cookies that were only on tantalizing display, but not for sale this morning. With considerable regret, I watched him zip his pants and fasten his belt. He snapped his watch into place. I sighed. He looked up and said, "Hi." This was the day we were going to pick up our airline tickets and visit a minister. We had been looking forward to it all week, planned on brunch at our favorite café and then maybe a walk along the harbor, where we'd seduce ourselves with talk of honeymoon beaches in Puerto Rico.

"I'm sorry, Jenny." He threaded the tie under his collar, then looped one end over the other. His tone was the tight, brisk one that tired people use to camouflage their exhaustion. "I . . ."

". . . have to go to work," I mumbled. My eyes drooped shut, and I burrowed back down into my pillow. "S'right." Our bed was a warm lake in which I was floating, and sleep was a rock tied to my foot; I was sinking beneath the surface of the water when his words revived me.

"I wish you'd get dressed and come with me."

"With you?" I struggled up onto both elbows. "Why?"

"Are you ready for this?" He pulled back the drapes at the window and raised the blinds, letting in a clatter of bright, thin November sunshine that hurt my eyes. I wasn't ready for that, or for the shock of his next words. "I want you to understand why I'm thinking of quitting the force."

"Quit?" I squinted at him through the pain in my eyes. "What?"

He transferred his wallet from the top of the dresser to his right back pocket and spoke to me as if he were continuing a conversation with himself. "It's not as if I have to work, I never had to work, you don't have to work. Hell, we could play Charles and Di on the combined incomes from our trust funds."

"No, thank you." I struggled to sit up.

"I woke up in the middle of the night, Jenny, and I paced around downstairs, thinking about it." He began to maneuver himself into a brown leather shoulder holster. "And I thought, what's a wealthy family for anyway, if not to support you in your disillusioned middle age? Hell, if I really wanted to work, I could join the family hardware business, sell frigging wrenches like my brothers, I don't need this damned cop work.''

''You always wanted to be a cop.''

He raised one shoulder, then the other, trying to shrug the holster into a position that would cause him the least discomfort. ''It ain't what it's supposed to be, Jenny.''

''What is?''

''You.'' He stared at me while he crooked his hands back and tugged down on the leather strap that crossed his back. ''Please, come with me this morning. I want you to understand, so you won't think I'm crazy. Or maybe so you'll know what's made me crazy, hell, I don't know.''

''What do you want me to do?''

''First, we'll talk to Eleanor Hanks.''

''Who?''

''The woman who killed her husband last night.''

I recoiled against the headboard. ''Geof, I don't want to.''

''Don't worry, she's not in jail,'' he said, misinterpreting my fear. ''She's not even under arrest yet, but it won't be long. After we get in the lab reports and the interviews, it'll close pretty quickly. And in the meantime, she's not going anywhere—no money, no relatives in town, three kids to take care of, she'll be there when we're ready for her.'' He picked up his gun from the dresser, checked it out, placed it in the holster. ''I'll clear it for you to talk to her.''

That was a lie: he wouldn't clear it, he'd just do it.

"I don't want to meet a woman who killed her husband."

He put his suit coat on, looked at me. "She's nice. You'll like her."

"She's *nice?* I'll *like* her?"

"I'm asking you. Please."

There wasn't really any choice, not if he was serious about wanting to quit the police force. I pushed back the covers, swung my feet over the bed and placed them on the carpet.

He patted the gun beneath his armpit and said, either to it or to me, "I do love you, lady." He walked out of the room then, only to reappear shortly afterward with fresh, hot coffee to prove the strength of his declaration. I was too upset to drink it—almost. This wasn't turning out to be any way I wanted to spend any Saturday morning in my life.

Eleanor Hanks had gathered her children the night before and gone to stay at Sunrise House, our local shelter for battered women. It wasn't actually a house, but rather a converted mom-and-pop grocery store in a neighborhood where the homeowners didn't have much more to lose in the way of property values. In the old days, the grocery was on the first floor, and the family who owned it lived upstairs. Now the second floor was a dorm for women and children, while the first floor had been divided by pasteboard wall partitions into kitchen, dining room, living room, and office. The Port Frederick Civic Foundation was a funder, so I was familiar with Sunrise House.

On the drive over, Geof didn't seem to want to talk except to briefly tell me a few more facts about the case. I kept myself from worrying about our future by working them into the morbid fantasy that I'd begun to weave in bed the night before. By the time we parked in front of the shelter, I'd played out the murder of Dick Hanks several times and several ways in my imagination, and some of it was beginning to settle in like truth, or memory.

Willie Henderson was waiting for us, leaning against the closed door of a clean brown sedan, working on his incisors with a toothpick. He, too, wore a suit (shiny green that caught the sun like algae on a pond), shirt (pale green), and a green-and-black-striped tie. Most Port Frederick cops, when they didn't wear uniforms, were given to conservative blues and browns.

Geof raised a hand to acknowledge Willie.

"You notice those black leather pants last night? He wore this green number his first day. Now some of them call him Liz. For Lizard."

"You think Willie crawled out from under a rock?"

"It's just the clothes, that's all."

Willie nodded back, then uncoiled himself, stuck the toothpick in his coat pocket, and strolled toward us. He had an odd gait, loose but stiff, like a runner who's warmed up and waiting for the gun. You had the feeling Willie could do wind sprints from a standing start.

"The Lizard was all right last night." Geof sounded grudging, but I decided it might only be weariness eating at the edges of his voice. "He doesn't talk much. He just kind of stands there and waits for his moment—like a lizard on a rock waiting for a fly to come by. Zap. Gotcha. He may work out all right, I don't know. It's a long way down from Boston to Port Frederick, though. We'll see if the fall bruised him."

I hoped I detected a future tense in that speech.

"I thought he jumped of his own free will," I said.

"He may have felt pushed by his wife's health. Either way, it's a long drop. It could be a hell of a blow to his wallet, not to mention his ego."

"Which seems, however, to be intact."

Geof was looking at me quizzically as Willie opened the door on my side.

I stepped out. "Thanks. Hello, Willie."

He looked across at Geof.

"She knows these people," Geof said, as if that explained my presence.

Willie nodded, apparently accepting the explanation.

I led the two men up the cracked cement walk to the door of the former grocery store.

"How 'bout you do the talkin'?" Willie suggested.

"This time," Geof agreed, making my heart lift with hope that he intended a next time. He was a good cop. He loved being a cop. Didn't he? This was all a mistake, a brief burnout. Wasn't it? How would I manage with an unemployed, depressed bridegroom?

I rang the doorbell, then stepped aside for the cops.

Soon, a female voice was raised on the other side of the door. "Yes? Who is it?"

"Police," Geof called back to her.

"Which ones?"

"Detectives Bushfield and Henderson, and Jenny Cain's here."

"Wait a minute, please." I knew that on the other side of that locked door a volunteer was running to get a staff member to get permission to open the door to us. Nobody, particularly men, ever got into Sunrise House without being checked out first—partly to protect the women's anonymity, partly to guard against the potential for violence from their abusive mates.

It was Smithy Leigh, the director, who opened the door to us.

"This wouldn't happen, Bushfield," she said at once, staring aggressively at Geof, "if you'd throw the bastards in jail for a year the first time you got called out on them."

"We only serve the law," he replied, smiling a little. "Smithy, this is Detective Willie Henderson. Willie, this is Smithy Leigh, the director of Sunrise House. She hates men, which she'll tell you is the natural result of accumulated evidence, but what the hell? Maybe you'll get a dispensation for being a member of an oppressed minority."

"Charming company you keep, Cain," she said to me.

"It's a dirty job," I agreed, eyeing Geof's profile, "but somebody's got to do it."

"I know you're here to see that poor Hanks woman," Smithy said, as if it were a dirty secret she had uncovered about us. "But I won't let you talk to her alone, get that? She doesn't have a lawyer yet, the poor silly twit doesn't seem to realize the situation she's in, and I won't have you badgering her unless I'm in the room."

I'd always kind of liked Smithy—or at least admired her—because she was as tough and fearless as a Rhodesian Ridgeback bitch in her protection of the wounded lambs of this world, but to my knowledge she'd never returned the compliment. At twenty-seven, she had a body like a rasp and a personality to match. Her pale, flat-featured face was surrounded by a mane of curly light brown hair that she never, on principle, combed. She had told me once that it was not on her agenda to attract the sexual attention of the enemy: men.

"Fine," Geof said, still smiling. "We'll only badger her when you're present."

She tightened her thin lips before saying in the grudging tones of a surrendering general, "She's upstairs with the kids. I'll bring her down. You three wait for me in the dining room."

We three had to open the door for ourselves, since she allowed it to slam in our faces.

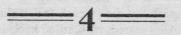

4

WE LET OURSELVES INTO THE SHELTER.

In the hall, a homely, chubby baby crawled across our path. He paused to gaze up in blue-eyed wonder at our great heights, and to drool a small pool of saliva onto the carpet.

"Shawnie, honey?"

From the adjoining living room, a teenager called out to the baby in the kind of high, sweet voice that no child ever obeys. The girl looked unformed, as if the sculptor had started the job by working the pale clay until it softened, and then left for lunch. She had a full-moon face, big breasts, spreading buttocks, and colorless hair that hung to her waist like unraveled rope. I remembered the room as the produce section of the old grocery store; she would have been sitting on the potatoes. In a pleading voice she crooned, "Come to Mommy, honey!"

The baby continued to stare up at the three strangers.

I felt the foolish grin that babies inspire spread across my face. When I looked at Geof, I saw it mirrored on him.

Willie leaned down and gave the little bottom a sharp swat.

"Git to your mama," he growled.

The child probably didn't even feel it through his diapers, but, looking scared, he scuttled back across the hall. There were three other small children in the living room and a fat black woman who had turned her face away from us when we came in.

Geof said to her, "Hello, Mrs. Gleason."

The black woman busied herself with one of the babies as she muttered, " 'Lo." We didn't move on, as Geof seemed to be waiting for something. Finally, Mrs. Gleason looked up, exposing a black and swollen left eye and a stitched gash at her temple; several of her front teeth were missing, so that when she spoke she sounded like an old woman. I bit my lower lip to keep my dismay to myself. She directed her words half defiantly, half apologetically at Geof: "He don't mean to do it, Officer Bushfield, he just gets drunk, you know him, that's all, and he ain't himself that way, but he don't never really mean to do it."

"It hurts you all the same."

She raised a hand to her wounded face but didn't touch it.

"It don't hurt," Mrs. Gleason said.

"Shit," Willie said under his breath.

The house and the people in it were making my stomach clench on the coffee I'd had for breakfast; there was such a palpable atmosphere of real and remembered pain, of

46

anger, shame, and an edginess that was expressed in darting glances, pinched mouths, sharp tones. I knew it wasn't always like this, I knew sometimes the house rang with laughter, and the faces shone with hope, real or imagined. But not this morning. And this was where they felt safe! The pity I felt for the children made me turn brusque.

"This way." I led the cops to the dining room.

They took chairs at the far end of a long wooden dining table that held dirty coffee cups and a baby's warming dish containing something that looked like crusted oatmeal. From the direction of the kitchen came the henhouse sound of women fixing breakfast together: chatter, scrabble, laughter, chatter. There was an aluminum coffeepot on a counter in the dining room, and some mugs that appeared clean, so I poured for us, and then I passed powdered cream and sugar to the men. I rummaged through the drawers until I came up with a single spoon, which I wiped off with my fingers, and held up to a light to examine.

"Cleanliness is not, contrary to popular opinion, a sex-linked trait," I remarked.

Satisfied that it might not spread ptomaine poisoning, I stuck the spoon in the sugar bowl. Then I unplugged the baby's warming dish, and stacked it and the dirty mugs on the counter. I swept crumbs off the table into my hand.

Geof said, "Are you going to do the laundry next, Jenny?"

I laughed weakly. "All right, I'll stop."

It was only motion for the sake of motion. I was nervous, not the least about meeting a woman the day after she killed her husband. I dumped the crumbs in a wastebasket and sat down between the men.

A woman I assumed to be Eleanor Hanks thrust herself into the room at that moment and collapsed into the first chair she came to. Immediately, my fantasy began to change. She was about ten pounds heavier than I'd imagined her and more attractive. I'd pictured a brunette, but this was a graying blonde, who looked as if she'd thrown on her clothes without looking at them, and then frantically patted her hair down. She stared at each of us in turn. Whatever she saw in our faces evidently caused her consternation, because first her lips quivered, then her face crumpled, and then she bent her head onto her folded arms on the table and began to cry, solidly and seriously as if she would never stop. Beside me, Willie muttered, "Shit."

"You remember we met last night, Mrs. Hanks," Geof said in a loud voice. "I'm Detective Geof Bushfield, this is Jenny Cain, and this fellow over here is Detective Willie Henderson. I know this is a terrible time for you, but you want to help us find out who killed your husband, isn't that right?"

He was the snake charmer playing his oily, hypnotic tunes of persuasion, and she was the captured cobra, one that had struck and killed, even if only after being tormented. Perform for us now, Eleanor! Rise from your dark basket of fears, uncoil those memories and truths, and spit them out at us! She looked so plain, so normal, so suburban. This woman, who resembled any dozen women I knew, had shot and killed a human being. I stared at Eleanor Hanks as tourists stare at exotic snakes in baskets—feeling sorry for their reduced circumstances, but wary of their latent, lethal power.

She suddenly stopped crying, as if she'd swallowed it whole. After a very quiet moment in which nobody moved, she nodded, then raised her face. I found myself looking at yet another discolored, swollen female face, although this damage might have been caused by the violence of her own weeping.

"Yes," she said in a whispery, shaky voice, "I want to help."

"Why don't you help *her*, Bushfield?" Smithy barged back into the dining room, jarring the atmosphere. She had a plate of bacon and eggs and a fork in her hands. "Tell her she needs a lawyer." She banged the plate down in front of her wounded lamb and stuck the fork in Eleanor Hanks's right hand. "You need a lawyer. Eat."

"Lawyer?" Mrs. Hanks looked blankly at Smithy, then at the fork, then across the table at Geof. The food might as well have been plastic for all the attention she paid to it.

"That's up to you," Geof said vaguely, smoothly. "We only have a few simple questions that we need to pursue in the course of our normal investigations."

Smithy grunted.

"Mrs. Hanks," Geof persevered, "would you tell us again about last night, please? And it would be helpful if you would be specific about times and places. Can you do that for me?"

"Yes," she whispered, and ducked her head once. "I think so."

"Good," Geof said warmly. Smithy compressed her lips and frowned at me as if demanding to know how I could associate with such a manipulative swine. "Let's begin about six o'clock last night. May I call you Eleanor?"

"Yes," she said obediently.

"Tell me what you were doing at six o'clock last night, Eleanor." Geof was folksy enough to be her neighbor. On the other side of me, Willie began taking unobtrusive notes on a pad on his lap, under the table.

"I was at work," she said promptly.

"Right," Geof said approvingly, as if she'd lived up to his high expectations of her. In his tone, there also was a hint, a warning: Right. You've told the truth. You've confirmed what we already know. And you'd be surprised how much we know, Eleanor, and how ready we are to trap you in a lie.

"And you left work . . . when?"

Her story, told with much crying and hesitancy, hardly matched my fantasy. Or was it her fantasy that didn't match reality?

Eleanor Hanks claimed that at about six-fifteen she left the fast-food restaurant where she worked as day manager. She said she drove to her neighborhood grocery store to pick up the weekend's supply of food for her family, then to the dry cleaner's to pick up a suit of her husband's, and then to a discount store for diapers, baby wipes, shampoo, and other dry goods that she said were too expensive at grocery store prices. Finally, she drove home, stopping one more time, to fill the car with gasoline, putting in the gas herself and paying cash "for the discount." By then it was, she estimated, nearly eight-thirty. She remembered feeling "kind of frantic," because she hadn't had anything to eat since noon, and she was running late for her once-a-month card game with "the girls."

She volunteered the information that when she got home, her husband was annoyed with her for not having fixed a casserole he could stick in the oven for his dinner. He complained that the baby had fussed, hadn't taken his bottle easily, was hard to put down. She said that while she took a shower, he sat on the lowered seat of the toilet grousing about his day in general and her failings in particular.

"Bad argument?" Geof asked sympathetically.

"Oh, it wasn't really an argument," she said quickly. "Dick was just in a bad mood, that's all."

"Did he yell at you?"

"Oh, no!"

"Did he hit you?"

"Oh, good heavens, no!"

"Where'd you keep the gun, Eleanor?"

"What? I didn't . . . Dick kept it in the drawer. Oh!"

She suddenly put her face in her hands and began to sob again. Smithy patted her forcefully on the back as if she were choking instead of crying. When she recovered, Geof resumed from another direction, simply asking her to continue telling us about her evening.

She claimed she got dressed, checked on the baby, and left Dick eating a sandwich in front of the television. What time was that? Nine-thirty or so. What time did she reach her friend's house? Nine forty-five. How long did she stay at the card party? Until after eleven-thirty, but it wasn't much of a party, nobody else showed up. But she stayed anyway? Oh, sure, it was her night out! She didn't leave and go home at any time before eleven-thirty? Oh, no. And when she got home, she found what? Her husband, lying in blood on the bedroom floor. She screamed when she saw him, embraced him, tried to revive him, screamed again at the blood that now covered the front of her clothes. More sobbing. Who was her friend? Lizbeth Miller, but Detective Bushfield had already asked her that last night, why did he need Lizbeth's name?"

"Because you need an alibi," Smithy said with brutal directness.

"Alibi . . ." Eleanor Hanks stared at us, her eyes wide, frightened, her mouth hanging slightly open. It was hard to believe she hadn't come to the same conclusion on her own, and much earlier. "Oh, no! Oh, I didn't! I didn't! Oh, my God in heaven, Lizbeth will tell you . . ." She thrust her face into her hands again, and the sobbing that seemed to come from some inexhaustible well of tears rose to hysteria. Smithy pulled Eleanor Hanks to her feet and forcefully propelled the sobbing woman back up the stairs. With her palms on Mrs. Hanks's back, Smithy turned her face toward me and mouthed, "Go away."

The women vanished onto the second floor.

"That poor woman," I murmured.

"You feelin' sorry for her?" Willie looked directly at me for the first time. "Maybe you want to remember, she ain't the one who's dead." He shifted his gaze back to Geof. "I talked to the Miller woman last night. Woke her up, pissed off her husband." Willie smiled slightly, as if the memory pleased him.

"And?"

"She says little old Eleanor sat right by her little old side all night long, until around eleven-thirty. Talkin'. And drinkin' Diet Pepsi." Willie was putting on a falsetto Southern accent that was deadly accurate, but not funny. "Why, honey, Eleanor and Dick got along just fine most of the time, why she just couldn't imagine who'd want to do such a terrible thing, but it surely wasn't little old Eleanor, she could surely vouch for that." Willie resumed speaking in his normal voice. "Mrs. Miller was as nervous as a Southern belle in a roomful of Yankee soldiers the whole time I talked to her."

"Being questioned in a murder case is enough to make anybody nervous," I suggested.

"Especially if they're lying," he retorted.

"Why are you so sure Mrs. Hanks killed him?"

He didn't even bother to reply this time, but only gave me a cynical, impatient look.

"Means," Geof explained, "motive, and opportunity, that's why. It's all too familiar, Jenny, it's just a classic case of domestic homicide." He led us back to the front door. "Willie, I have a couple of things to do with Jenny, but I'll be back to the station in half an hour."

Willie nodded to me before walking off toward his car.

I felt like crawling back into bed and closing my eyes to this vision of the world that revealed black eyes, sobbing women, cynical cops, and dead men. It was a relief to get out of Sunrise House.

"All right," I said to Geof when we were back in his car. "That was awful, but it wasn't any worse than a lot of other cases. So what is it, exactly, about this one?"

"It's not just this one." He turned the key in the ignition. "There's more."

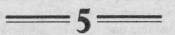

5

WE DROVE AWAY FROM THE SHELTER.

In a grim voice, Geof said, "We were going to look at houses today, and that's what we're going to do. They just won't be any houses we'd want to live in."

It turned out to be a strange, sad homes tour.

A few blocks from Sunrise House, he pulled over to the curb and pointed. "Look at that stone house with the loose gutters."

I did that.

"Once upon a time," he said, "there was a mommy and a daddy and five children. Daddy broke Mommy's jaw, one of her arms and a couple of her fingers, not all at the same time, you understand, and not necessarily in that order. There was a miscarriage, too, that seemed suspicious to us. We've been called out something like twenty times in the past three or four years to that little stone house. His name is James, her name is Lanny, they're about twenty-five years old. Every Saturday afternoon they let the kids go to her mother's, and they sit in that house and get drunk as two lords. He gets drunk because he's an alcoholic; I think she gets drunk for anesthetic, so it won't hurt so much when he beats her. She's left him several times, and she won't ever say why she goes back to him, but I suspect it's because he threatens her, or the children, or maybe her mother.''

I wanted him to drive quickly away from that house before its unhappiness infected us. Judging from the strain in his voice and the stoic set of his mouth, it had already sickened him.

Ours is a small city, and so I asked the obvious: ''Do I know them?''

''You saw her this morning.''

''Which?''

''Mrs. Gleason, the black one.''

''*She's* twenty-five years old?''

''Nobody knows the trouble she's seen,'' he said, wryly. ''That little stone house over there could be the scene of a murder, Jenny—it just hasn't happened yet, that's all. But one of these nights we could find one dead Gleason, or two, and maybe the children. That depends on how desperate she gets or how crazy he gets.'' He shifted the car back into drive. ''Okay, you've seen this one. Let's go.''

''I can hardly wait.'' I gazed out the windshield and spoke to an imaginary person seated on the hood of the car: ''And what did you and your fiancé do to get ready for your wedding day, Jenny? You probably had a lot of fun going to parties and picking out china and planning your honeymoon. Oh, no, actually we interviewed a woman who'd just killed her husband, and we met another couple of abused women, and then we drove around town and watched marriages disintegrate. It's fun, really, it ought to be required of every young couple, like a blood test.''

''I'm sorry.'' He reached over to stroke my cheek with the back of his fingers.

''Good.'' I kissed his knuckles. ''Now that I've got that out of my system . . .''

We drove past three other homes where fate sat like a malevolent fat man on the front stoop, gorging on the violence, waiting for either the husband or wife to open the door for the final feast and say, ''It's time. Come in.''

Finally, we parked in front of a white frame one-story house on the corner of a block of similar homes.

''That's the Hanks house,'' Geof told me, unnecessarily, since that fact was obvious from the presence of the two police cars in the driveway and the wide plastic ribbon that surrounded the property and marked it as a crime scene: do not enter, danger, forbidden. ''This is where it happened last night, Jenny.''

It was much like the house of my imagination—small, ordinary. I pictured her driving into the garage, parking, pausing wearily; only now I had a real face to put on the woman of my fantasy, a worn, sad, tired, confused, hiding face.

''Now.'' I turned to face Geof. ''Tell me.''

He sighed, shrugged, and suddenly looked every bit as tired as the real Eleanor Hanks and the one in my imagination. ''I'm sick of losing this game, Jenny. It used to be I felt sorry for the women, and maybe even a little compassion for the men, but not anymore, I just mostly feel sick of all of them. I'm losing my patience with the women, and I'm ready to throw the men through brick walls. I'm so sick of these domestic cases I could puke, and this Hanks business just tops it. It just goddamn tops it.''

"Why?"

"Maybe . . . because I knew them." He said it hesitantly, as if he were still working it out in his own mind. His eyes seemed to look inward, as if he were reviewing mental photographs and finding them disturbing. "It's a funny thing, Jenny, but in police work you get to know a lot of people, not well, but intimately. I wouldn't have recognized either one of them if I'd seen them on the street, and yet I knew one of their most intimate and awful family secrets, which was the fact that he beat her up. I knew it, Jenny, I'd been called out to that house twice, and I still didn't do a damn thing to prevent this from happening."

"Didn't, or couldn't?"

"It may have been couldn't, but it feels like didn't."

"I don't believe this responsibility belongs to you."

"I think part of it does."

There was a police-issue shotgun between us that kept me from sliding across to embrace him, so I had to settle for placing my hand against his face. "So you're going to quit."

Something that looked like pain appeared in his eyes.

"It's funny, isn't it? I'll bet I've seen a thousand domestic disturbances, but it's number one thousand and one that finally gets to me. Hell, Jenny, I don't want to be one of those cops who's so numb he doesn't give a damn. I'd rather quit first. But listen." He took my hands in his and squeezed. "I don't want you to worry about this." He blinked and then laughed suddenly, wryly. "Listen to me. Here, we're getting married in two weeks, and I tell you I hate my job and I'm going to quit, and then I say, hey, don't worry about it. Christ. I sound like the cheating husband who confesses to his wife because it makes him feel so much better.''

"You don't have anything else to tell me, do you?''

"Not along those lines.'' He tried to smile, a brave attempt that wrung my heart. "No, you only have to marry me, you don't have to be my psychotherapist. I just want you to understand what's going on with me, that's all. I don't expect you to fix it. Anyway, it's only a job, it's not the end of the world. I'll tell you what . . . maybe I'll get finished early enough so that we can still see that minister today. All right? You want to?''

"Sure.''

But it wasn't all right.

Suddenly, nothing was.

He dropped me off at home on his way back to the station. When I walked in, the phone was ringing. I thought about ignoring it, but changed my mind, picked it up, and said hello.

"So, *get* married without telling your own sister.''

"Sherry.'' I tried to sound glad to hear from my only sibling.

"Tell everybody else, but don't—''

"We've hardly told anybody, so how'd you—''

"You told Dad,'' she said accusingly.

I slumped onto the stool by the phone and tried to rise from Geof's depths to her superficiality without getting the bends.

"Well, yes, we had to let him know early enough so he'd get airplane reservations, but—''

"So what do I need to do, move out of town to find out?'' My little sister's humor was the sharp, pointed kind that some women throw out ahead of themselves defensively, like spears. "You'd better not expect me to be matron of honor, because I don't have time to shop for a dress.''

''I don't.''

''Oh. Well, I *can* manage to have a wedding shower for you, although I certainly would have appreciated a little advance notice, like two months in advance instead of two weeks! I've been thinking about it ever since Dad called, and here's what I want you to do—get me a list of twenty-five of your friends by this afternoon and I'll mail the invitations tonight. We can't have it during the week because that's not enough time, and anyway, we've got a ball game Monday night, and Lars has his tennis on Tuesday, and I've always got church guild on Wednesday nights. We'll have it next Saturday night over here at our house. I thought about having it at our club, but considering some of your friends . . .''

''Send me your poor,'' I murmured, ''your blacks, your gays, your huddled masses yearning to breathe free.''

''Not to *our* club,'' she snapped, and I found myself smiling at the phone. ''Lars wants to come, too, so that means we'll have to include the men. We might as well, anyway, I mean you're not exactly some innocent young virgin.''

''You make it sound like human sacrifice, Sherry.''

''Oh, you're so naive.'' Her sigh was that of the experienced married woman. ''What do you think marriage is, Sis? I'll tell you what it is—some man wraps love around your eyes like a blindfold, he binds your hands with sex, then he leads you to the altar to sacrifice your brains to his ambition and your abilities to his convenience. You don't think he's going to cook after you marry him, do you?''

''You went willingly enough when you married Lars.''

''Lars is different.'' That was true, Lars Guthrie was

different—any man who could live with Sherry for ten years was either tough as granite, pliable as plastic, or dumb as a post. "What I'm saying, Jenny, is this shower can't be one of those giggly girlish things where you play those stupid games like how many other words can you make out of the word 'divorce.' You're too *old;* that would be absurd. I suppose we'll have it catered, maybe a sea-food buffet, God knows you haven't given me enough notice to fix anything myself. And I think we'll open the bar instead of doing some insipid punch. Do you want gifts? If we don't say, and we invite the men, you're likely to get some pretty raunchy . . ."

"No gifts. No party."

That stopped her for one second.

"This isn't for you, Jenny." My sister had a small, straight, perfect nose down which she viewed the world's population of lesser mortals. She was talking down it now. "These parties are never for the bride, they're for the married friends of the bride who want to push you into that great sticky vat of marriage in which they're already mired."

"Sherry, you're so articulate."

"Thank you."

"But you have so little to say."

"As I started to *say,* it would be unkind of you to deny us that pleasure! So don't get the idea I'm doing any of this for you. Or for that former juvenile delinquent you're marrying. I won't say you could have had anyone, Jenny, but you might have managed a stockbroker or even a lawyer. How do you think I'll feel having to introduce my brother-in-law the cop?"

"Safer," I said. "My friends don't want a party, either."

"If you don't send me a list of your friends, I'll invite my own. God knows, I'd rather."

"There's a lot to be said for being an only child."

"I need that list ASAP," Sherry Cain Guthrie informed me crisply and hung up.

I drew toward me a pad and pencil and thought a moment.

So she wanted a list. Okay, I'd give her a list.

Smiling malignantly to myself, I made my first entry: "Detective and Mrs. Willie J. Henderson." I thought next of an irascible professor, Henry Ingram, and his wife, Kathy, who was thirty years younger than he. A couple of other cops. And maybe Smithy Leigh would be so shocked to receive an invitation that she'd accept it. And I knew a beautiful black social worker named Sabrina Johnson and a gay psychologist named Tommy Nichol who'd get a kick out of observing the tribal rituals of white Anglo-Saxon Protestant heterosexual suburbanites.

Within a few minutes, my little sister had her guest list, all right, and not a socially acceptable name among them. As I looked it over, cackling in an unseemly manner, I realized that, among the twenty-five guests, I'd included a veritable panel of experts on the subject of domestic violence: one director of a home for battered women, one psychologist who counseled perpetrators, one social worker, a couple of social scientists who specialized in the subject, and several cops. The list wasn't much of a coincidence, either, since my Foundation work often took me into the world of social services.

A panel of experts. On domestic violence.

"I don't expect you to fix it," Geof had said.

But as the director of a charitable foundation, and by nature, I was an incorrigible "fixer." The Foundation. God knows, the Port Frederick Civic Foundation liked to fix and build and save things. It liked to fix broken budgets, save historical landmarks, build theaters and hospital wings. It liked to provide hot lunches for the elderly, shoes for the ballet, trumpets for the band, counseling for pregnant women. So why not a coalition of community advisers to investigate the causes of domestic violence in this town?

I began to look up some phone numbers.

The rest of the day passed quickly. The illusion of solving problems will do that, every time.

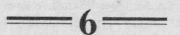

SATURDAY NIGHT, AND NO PLACE TO GO.

With Geof working on the Hanks homicide that night, it looked as if it was going to be me, the refrigerator, and the telephone. After living with him for so long, I was used to it. Or should have been. But if I was so used to it, why was I making two trips every half hour to raid the refrigerator, starting with celery stalks at five-thirty and working my way up to Sara Lee banana cake by eight?

At eight-five, I put my fork down.

"No offense, Sara, but as sublimation, you suck."

I walked my plate to the sink and washed the remains of beige cake and yellow icing down the disposal. Then I returned to my other date, the telephone.

"Gail?" I said, when Willie's wife answered on the third ring. "It's Jenny Cain. I'm just sitting here by myself gaining weight, and I wondered if you and the kids could stand some company tonight?'' There was a pause before she coughed, then said with no perceptible enthusiasm, ''That would be fine, Jenny. Come on over.''

''If you're busy . . .''

''No, I'd like you to meet the kids.''

''I'd like that, too. I'll leave soon.''

''Fine,'' she said, and hung up.

I spoke to the dial tone: ''Sara Lee loves me.''

If Gail wasn't in any hurry for company, I wouldn't rush over there. Maybe I'd stop by the station to see Geof. Maybe I'd call her from there and offer to pick up a pizza in order to buy myself a warmer welcome on a lonely Saturday night. And maybe this would turn out to be a good time to spring my idea of the coalition on Geof.

The Port Frederick police station looks as if it ought to be a fire station. It's an old, deep, narrow red brick building with a front door like the mouth of a cave, four stories, and a police garage in the basement. The detectives are housed at the top in a plain gray warren of offices on which the taxpayers do not waste money on curtains or pictures on the walls. The decor runs to gray metal desks, green metal swivel chairs, beige metal file cabinets, old typewriters, new telephones, bare wooden floors, fluorescent lights, and dirty white walls. Geof often called it, not entirely ironically, his little piece of paradise. Walking into it on that Saturday night, I could not imagine it without him.

''Jenny?'' The man himself stepped out of his cubicle of an office with file folders in his hands, and suddenly the room was handsomely decorated. If I had been a suspect, I would have volunteered to cooperate in any way he suggested. "Damn, if I'd known you were coming up, I'd have asked you to pick up a pizza."

"Pizza?" Across the room, three cops looked up.

"No." I smiled at them. "Sorry."

"Come on in." Geof stepped aside to let me pass through into his office where Willie Henderson sat hunched over Geof's desk, perusing computer printouts. "I'll be back in a minute."

"What kind of pizza?" Willie asked, without looking up.

"It's only a rumor," I said. "What's new, Willie?"

"Dick Hanks was shot with a .38," he said in the flat tone of a man talking to himself. I slid quietly into an empty chair, and listened. "And it just happens the college issued a .38 to him when he took the security job, and it just happens that gun is missing from the house. We found two slugs. He was shot once in the chest and once in the face."

"That's pretty accurate," I observed.

"Yeah, if we find out she's been practicing at some gun range, she can kiss self-defense good-bye. She used a pillow to muffle the noise. She says she doesn't know where the gun is now." He snorted. "Right. Like I don't know where my car's parked." The lines in his high forehead deepened when he frowned. "We had two, maybe three, cases in Boston where there was a D.H., and we never found the gun. We knew the wife did it. Knew it, goddamn we knew it, but we never could prove it. Sometimes they just get away with it. Jesus, it pisses me off when that happens. I'm gonna be pissed if it happens this time."

"What about powder traces, Willie?"

Inwardly, I smiled: living with a cop had given me some pretty strange conversational gambits.

"Gloves, probably, and she tossed them, too."

"Gloves? That would imply premeditation, wouldn't it?"

"The whole thing implies premeditation. Her *denial* implies it."

That sounded like a Catch-22 to me.

"What do you think happened, Willie?"

"I think she was plannin' to off him and just waiting for the right time to do it. I think she went to the card party, all right, and when she saw that none of the other ladies showed up, she saw her chance. I think she cooked up her alibi with her pal Lizbeth, and then she left early and went home and shot him. Then she disposed of the gun and the gloves, and then she worked herself up into a nice believable hysteria, and then she called us." I wondered if this conversation meant acceptance. Or, maybe crime was the one thing that got Willie talking. "It wasn't a burglary. And we haven't found anybody but her who had a reason to want to kill him. He's dead, and she's it."

"You don't have much sympathy for her."

"Like I said, she ain't the one who's dead."

He looked past me, out into the squad room where Geof was standing. Willie jerked his head in Geof's direction. "If he's been a cop so long, how come he's never made rank?"

"He's never wanted to sit behind a desk. They've offered promotions, Willie, but he's always turned them down."

"Weird," Willie grunted, and returned to his printouts.

I shrugged, though he didn't see me. "It makes sense to him." Or, at least it used to, I thought. I let Willie work in silence while I brooded over that for a few minutes. Finally, I said, "Willie, I'm going to your house when I leave here."

He frowned at me over his shoulder. "What for?"

I shrugged again. "Something to do."

Geof stepped back into the office, looking like a man who could have used a week of sleep, and I forgot about calling Gail.

"We got the pictures back." He dumped a file folder in front of Willie, who picked it up and moved it off his printouts. Geof walked over to me, leaned down, placed his hands on the chair arms on either side of me, and started to kiss me.

"Hey," Willie said. "Stop that."

Geof finished the kiss and rubbed his forehead against mine. "Lucky Jenny. Another thrilling Saturday night in the life of a cop's wife."

"I'm not a wife yet."

He smiled tiredly. "Is that a threat?"

"Not on your life, buster, I'll see you at the church, if not sooner. Oh, God, it has to be sooner—Sherry wants to throw a party for us next Saturday night. I'm sorry, but I guess we'll have to—"

"That's nice," he said, standing up straight again.

"Nice? You think that's nice?"

"Sure." He grabbed the folder Willie had pushed aside and began to shuffle through the large photographs it contained. He glanced at me. "I'm glad, I think it's great. These are the Hanks crime scene. You want to see?"

"No," I said firmly. But then, thinking he was pretty great, too, to put up so cheerfully with my family, I reached for the crime scene photographs. I had the curiosity, all right, but not the stomach for it. Still, I forced myself, as if it were some kind of yogic exercise in self-discipline, to stare at the pictures of Dick Hanks's body, and of the bedroom where he'd been shot, and of Eleanor Hanks's bloody clothes lying in a heap on the bathroom floor. She must have changed before the cops arrived.

There was something to be said for the old days, I thought, when crime photographs were, of necessity, in black and white. These were all too vividly colored—the red on her short knit skirt had soaked through to her bikini panties, there was red covering her deep-V jersey top, and it had splattered onto her high heels and hose. It might have looked sexy on the cover of a pulp magazine, but I felt my stomach contract.

Geof noticed that I was staring into space.

"What do you think?"

I told him, then added, "In addition, I've brought you something better than pizza."

"Thanks." He took the photographs from me and smiled in a distracted way. "But you already heard Willie say they don't allow that in the office, Jenny."

"Geof." I cleared my throat and hoped I wouldn't have to clear my foot out of it, as well. "I spent a good deal of this afternoon talking to experts in the field of domestic violence."

He shifted his gaze from the photos to me.

"And I've been thinking," I continued, "that the Foundation might bring all of you together as a coalition of experts to figure out solutions to the problem."

He looked at me as if I'd suggested a manned space flight to the sun. "I already know the solutions to domestic violence, Jenny, and there are only two of them: death and divorce."

Without looking up, Willie laughed.

"You don't believe that," I suggested.

"What do you think I've been trying to tell you?"

I stood and feigned nonchalance. "Well, at two o'clock on Monday afternoon, there will be social workers, a couple of research scientists, and a psychologist in my office to discuss the problem of domestic violence in Port Frederick, Massachusetts. It would be nice to have representatives of the police there, as well, but that's up to you.''

I smiled at him, and affected what is known as a breezy exit.

When I was halfway to the outer door, he yelled across the squad room: *"I'd rather have pepperoni!"*

Across the room, a cop looked up and said, "Pizza?"

I stood on the front porch of the Hendersons' rented house, cradling a sausage pizza, and rang the bell with my elbow.

Nobody answered by the fifth ring.

I had tried to call her from the pizza place, but her phone had been continually busy. She must have gotten tired of waiting for me, I thought, and taken her kids somewhere. This was a fine way to start a friendship.

"I'm sorry," I said to the closed front door.

I looked around for a note, but she hadn't left one, so I took a pen from my purse and scribbled an apology on the warm box. Then I placed the pizza in front of the door, thinking she could warm it up and have it for lunch the next day. I hoped the kids wouldn't step on it in the dark.

After that, I went home and finished off the Sara Lee banana cake.

Geof slid into bed after I was asleep.

"Mmm?" I said, waking.

He pulled me over to him so that my head rested in the hollow of his shoulder.

"I might as well have stayed home."

"No case?"

"No confession, no weapon, no witness. And no other suspects, either. God, I wish that baby could talk."

I slapped his chest lightly with my fingers. "No, you don't."

"From the police point of view, I do."

"Any point of view that would have a child be a witness to his mother killing his father sounds pretty limited to me."

"I've been telling you I need a new point of view."

"If you quit, what will you do instead?"

"Hell, I don't know. Become a private investigator. And then I'd get to handle dirty domestic cases, which is exactly what I need, right? Night watchman? Security guard? Law school?"

"You hated school."

He laughed shortly. "Right. So maybe I'll call my family's bluff and join the firm."

"You'd have to move."

This time his sigh took my hand even farther into the air, then down again. "Right, and your job's here. Well, what do you think I ought to do, Jenny?"

"For the short-term, how about this?" I raised my head and kissed the warm hollow where it had lain. Then I strung a rosary of kisses along his collarbone, moved up behind his ear, over to his temple, down to his mouth. But within a few minutes it became clear that he wasn't going to be able to follow through on that suggestion, either.

"I'm sorry," he repeated.

I settled back down into the hollow of his shoulder.

"Don't worry about it, honey. You're tired, that's all."

He hugged me closer to him, but then released me as if that small action had expended all his energy.

"Yes," he said too quietly. "I am."

The next day, when Geof had returned to the station, I called the minister at the local nondenominational church to explain that we wouldn't be coming in for the usual premarital counseling.

"You can't find the time?" There was a note of polite disbelief in his resonant preacher's voice.

"I can," I explained. "He can't."

"It often happens that men are reluctant to commit the time to discussing matters of the heart," he said, sounding both angry and sad about it.

"No, that's not it."

"Marriage itself takes time, you know."

He was trying to be helpful and cautionary, but it only succeeded in making me feel annoyed and defensive. We'd agreed to a church wedding only as a sentimental gesture to please our families.

"I promise he'll show up at the church," I said.

"I hate to say it, but sometimes, when they're reluctant to begin with, it's better if they don't."

"This is not one of those times."

"Well, of course, I don't really know either of you." He managed to sound both appeasing and accusing. By the time we hung up, I was having serious doubts. About sentimental gestures.

7

AT TWO O'CLOCK ON MONDAY AFTERNOON, I TRIED TO convene the first meeting of the coalition on domestic violence. It wasn't easy. Seated around the conference table at the Foundation office was an animated, chattering group that included, counterclockwise from where I stood at the head of the table: Sabrina Johnson, a beautiful black social worker who looked as if she ought to be modeling for *Vogue;* Tommy Nichol, a young psychologist who counseled batterers and who also happened to be gay; Smithy Leigh, the director of Sunrise House; Geof, who looked as if he'd rather be elsewhere; Willie Henderson, who looked as if he'd like to be there, too; and Dr. Henry Ingram and his wife, Kathy, who were social scientists whose special field of research was domestic violence.

I stood up and cleared my throat.

It didn't have the slightest effect.

"Well, of course she did it," Henry Ingram was saying impatiently to his wife, a round, dark-haired plum of a woman who was a good thirty years younger than he. Henry removed his unlit cigar from his mouth long enough to add, "And good riddance to bad rubbish, I say."

"Oh, Henry," Kathy said, sighing, as she often did.

"Do you have any evidence to support that accusation?" Smithy demanded from across the table. With her hunched shoulders and her mass of uncombed hair, she brought to mind a drab brown shrub.

"It's perfectly obvious, Ms. Leigh."

"So is slander!"

"Oh, Henry."

"Married!" Sabrina Johnson was leaning toward Tommy, who was grinning up at me. She was my age, thirty-three, but that's where most similarities ended. I'm tall, but Sabrina was an all-American basketball player at Boston College and still moved with an athlete's grace. On this day she was wearing skintight blue jeans tucked into cowboy boots and an oversize man's sweater that looked like Paris on her. She had her long, wild black hair snatched back behind her ears by barrettes. "Can you believe they're tying the knot, after all this time? Or is it a noose?" She turned and joined Tommy in grinning at me. "What is this, Jenny, another triumph of faith over reason?"

"May I take a date to the party, Jenny?" Tommy asked.

"Sure," I said, nodding helplessly, though it did give me a moment's malicious pleasure to imagine my sister's reaction when Tommy walked into her house with another man. I tried again. "People? Excuse me?"

At the far end of the table, Geof was leaning back in his chair, his hands in his pants pockets, taking it all in. I caught his eye, and he smiled slightly.

"Thank you for coming," I said loudly.

"You're welcome!" Sabrina called back, causing everybody else to laugh, even Henry Ingram and Willie. In a more normal tone, she said, "But tell us again, Jenny, why are we here? I need another committee like I need a tan." She laughed again, along with the others.

"Because the Foundation is forming a coalition of community advisers to look for causes and solutions to the problem of domestic violence in this city," I said quickly. "As you know, there was a domestic homicide in Port Frederick over the weekend—"

There were nods, exchanges of glances.

"—and, while we might not have been able to do anything to prevent that tragedy, maybe we can work together to help prevent similar ones."

"We all knew the Hankses," Sabrina said. "Right, folks?"

Everybody except Willie nodded again.

"Then you probably feel as I do," I continued, "that we don't want anything like that to happen again, if we can prevent it. This is a community, after all, and whatever happens to any one of us affects the rest of us. So. You are the logical people to address this issue, because in one way or another, you're all experts on the subject."

"Experts!" Sabrina grinned. "Will you listen to that?"

"For example," I persevered, "Tommy, here, counsels the perpetrators, that is, the men who do the hitting. Sabrina sees a lot of the victims and their families in her office at social welfare. Smithy, of course, offers shelter at Sunrise House. Henry and Kathy, whose research is funded in part by this Foundation, have been studying domestic violence for years, so they're uniquely qualified to advise us. As for the detectives, they pick up the pieces and try to keep families from killing each other. That's Willie J. Henderson, by the way, who's new to our force, from Boston.''

"Of course he's from Boston," Sabrina said, wryly, knowingly. I liked Sabrina a great deal, but conducting a meeting around her could sometimes be as trying as guarding her on a basketball court. "Everybody in Massachusetts is from Boston at one time or another!"

I smiled, nodded. "So, if you're agreeable to the idea of working together, we'll get started."

Smithy Leigh's hand flew up to get my attention, and I saw that she'd merely been simmering, waiting her chance to boil over. "I don't know what else you expect us to do, Cain." She glared around the table, daring us to contradict her. "We're doing the best we can, but we're only one little shelter, for God's sake. What more do you expect us to do!"

"You do wonderful work," I soothed, "but you're the emergency ward, Smithy, and we're talking about preventive medicine. If we're effective, you'll see fewer 'patients.' "

"How?" Uncharacteristically, she cracked a joke, although maybe she didn't mean it to be funny. "Is this coalition going to kill all the men in town?"

Sabrina laughed. "I might vote for that."

"Committees!" Henry Ingram snapped.

"I'm hoping for a less drastic solution," I admitted, then I added, firmly, trying like hell to maintain some semblance of control over this rowdy group, "Let's begin by asking the Ingrams to talk about the root causes of domestic violence, all right?''

Heads nodded, and I sat down, letting out a sigh.

Kathy Ingram looked at Henry.

He sighed, too, but removed his cigar from his mouth again.

''Assuming,'' he said in a lofty, lecturing tone, ''we are talking about more or less normal people, and not about a true psychopath or sociopath, it is not merely an individual, but also a societal problem.''

I was heartened to see Geof lean forward to listen.

Henry, tall and stooped, as if he were forever going through doors that were too short for him, had an odd voice, deep and rumbling but with a touch of whine to it, like a truck in a tunnel. It made even his most superficial comments sound profoundly pessimistic. As he continued with his lecture, I had a sudden overwhelming urge to turn on more lights in the room. ''It is, to some degree, a holdover from male-dominated societies,'' he said. ''These men believe they have the right, even the obligation, to dictate to women what they may do, say, wear, be. These men blame the women for the beatings. They see no fault in themselves, although they may experience enormous guilt afterward. Even then, however, they will blame their own guilt and misery on the woman—''

''That's right!'' Tommy Nichol interrupted from across the table, much to Henry's obvious displeasure. With his rounded shoulders and his pudgy torso, which was set on thin legs that descended to pigeon toes, Tommy always reminded me of an ice-cream cone. On this day, he was wearing, besides a white shirt and beige trousers, the earnest expression of the social worker who's still too new at his job to be disillusioned. Tommy was practically bouncing in his chair in his eagerness to agree with Henry. Sabrina and I exchanged hidden smiles. "In my group counseling, they say, 'I hated to hit her, I begged her to act right! If she would only do what I tell her to, I wouldn't have to hit her!'"

"Bastards!" Smithy said between tightened lips.

"It is a question of power and dominance," Henry continued, ignoring the interruptions. At the age of seventy-four, and with his personality and national reputation, he tended to dominate any group, a factor I had considered before inviting him into the coalition. He was saying, "And it is nearly identical to the rationalization that goes through the mind of a parent who hits a child." He cleared his throat. "Kathy will now explain about the correlation between domestic violence and social conditions."

He stuck his cigar back in his mouth.

Kathy Ingram looked startled, but she recovered quickly and took up the lecture where her husband had left off.

"Domestic violence frequently accompanies unstable social conditions," she began. As opposed to Henry, everything Kathy said sounded comforting, like a mother's soothing murmurs, even when the words themselves were disturbing. "When a business closes, for example, men lose their jobs, their debts mount, their self-esteem suffers, they have too much idle time on their hands, their troubles multiply—"

"That's true!" Tommy Nichol broke in excitedly. "Then it gets to them, and they pour alcohol on the problem, and then they lose control of themselves—"

"And then they whomp the missus," Sabrina concluded dryly.

Kathy looked pained at Sabrina's unscientific choice of

words. "Substance abuse, whether alcohol or drugs, frequently plays a role in domestic violence, but it is not always a factor, Sabrina. Some people, and not just men, I would add, can become extremely violent when they are sober."

"Dick Hanks was a lush," Smithy said, abruptly.

"Surely that's confidential information," Kathy objected.

"Oh, Kathy!" It was Sabrina's turn to be comforting. "Everybody knew that. Even I knew it, and I'd never met the man. But she was in my office a couple of times, inquiring about government funds, and once, when she was really upset, she talked about his drinking. Wasn't he in one of your groups, Tommy?"

"No." Tommy Nichol shook his head regretfully and glanced at Geof. "I tried to get him interested in coming, after Detective Bushfield told me they had troubles, but Dick Hanks was really into denial, and he was furious when I called him and even hinted at the problem. I was afraid he was going to sue me, or something, just for mentioning it."

I noticed that Geof and Willie were listening very closely to these exchanges. I also noticed that I seemed to be practically the one person in the room who hadn't been acquainted with the Hankses. Evidently the social services network had reached out and tried to help them. And failed. Could we hope to do any better with anybody else?

"As I said before," Henry Ingram interjected, "good riddance to bad rubbish!"

"Henry!" Kathy turned to him again. "You don't mean that! Think of those poor children if she goes to jail—"

"Katherine," he argued, "you know perfectly well

that woman won't see a year in jail. She'll plead the Battered Wife Syndrome and—"

"That's no guarantee!" Smithy said angrily.

"Well, she will," Henry maintained. "It's the only logical thing for her to do, damn fool woman."

"Henry," I couldn't help but say, "if you think his death was good riddance to bad rubbish, and you think she did it, then why is she a damn fool woman?"

He grimaced. "Because she didn't do it sooner."

Smithy startled me with a sudden burst of laughter.

"Oh, Henry." Kathy sighed.

"Uh," I said, realizing belatedly that I had once again lost control of the meeting, "how about a public education campaign?"

". . . and thanks for coming."

By the time we adjourned—with plans for a "family peace" program in the schools and a training program for police officers and a media campaign and a crisis hotline—most of the members of the new task force seemed hopeful that we might eventually do some good for the battling families of our town.

The only ones who still looked skeptical were Dr. Henry Ingram and the two cops. That was unfortunate, since my original reason for sponsoring the meeting was less noble than it might have seemed, having less to do with solving other people's domestic problems than with preventing my own.

"Jenny?"

It was Kathy Ingram, touching my sleeve as I gathered my papers at the head of the conference table. I looked down into her soft, gentle, intelligent face. Only ten years separated our ages, and yet Kathy had always seemed to me like somebody's old-fashioned aunt. Partly it was the way she dressed—as on this day, in a blue-and-white patterned shirtwaist dress buttoned to the throat, with a gold pin in the shape of a pine tree on her white collar. She always made me think of doilies and sweet sherry; she was gracious, like a hostess, and kind. I liked her; there was no reason not to, but she never came to mind when I wanted to ask a friend to lunch. And I couldn't imagine ever having a couple of beers at The Buoy with Kathy Ingram. Friendship requires a little mutual bitching, a little mutual telling of secrets, and Kathy never complained or confided. I sometimes wondered if marriage to a much older man had turned her prematurely mature, or if she'd been born middle-aged. Kathy might have been only forty-four, but she wasn't young anymore, if she had ever been.

"I'm sorry about Henry." She was whispering, like a nurse who's afraid of waking the patient. "His blood pressure is up, and you know how he is when that happens. He's upset anyway, because of that poor Dick Hanks." At the questioning look on my face, she added, looking distressed, "We interviewed Dick and Eleanor a couple of times . . . after they came to the attention of the social welfare system. And it's, well, it's upsetting. I'm afraid we take these things more personally perhaps than good scientists ought to do."

"I understand, Kathy."

"He'll be better next time," she whispered, as a nurse might about her obstreperous charge. "I'll see that he takes his medicine."

I had been bending over to hear her. It was a relief to my neck and back when she finally scurried down the hall after her husband.

Geof had been waiting at a discreet distance, peering

out a window. Now he strolled over to me, his hands in his pants pockets.

"Nice try, Jenny," he said. "I don't know if it'll do any good."

"Give it a chance."

He kissed me lightly. "We'll see."

Sabrina caught me as I came out the door from the conference room. She grabbed my elbow, and bent over to whisper in my ear: "Is that other cop married?"

"Very. With two kids, and a third on the way."

I wouldn't have picked Willie for her type, and told her so.

Her perfect lips lifted in a wry smile. "History would suggest I'm not all that particular, Jenny." She gazed at me thoughtfully for a moment, as if she were trying to make up her mind about something. Finally, she said, the smile turning a little bitter, "You're getting more of an expert here than you know, pal. I used to be married to a guy who beat up on me a few times." She shrugged, but it turned into something more like a shiver. "When I hear about women like Eleanor Hanks, I always think, there but for the grace of God—"

She said good-bye and loped out the door.

Even Sabrina wasn't, I discovered a moment later, actually the last person to leave. Smithy Leigh was waiting for me in the outer office, looking as uncomfortable as she always did when she had to ask a favor.

"You've got a lot of contacts," she said bluntly. "And I've got a young woman staying at the shelter who thinks everything's going to be okay"—Smithy rolled her eyes toward the ceiling, cynically—"if her husband could only find a job."

I thought of the fat black woman who looked so much older than her years. "Mrs. Gleason?"

"No," Smithy said, "another one."

"What do you want me to do?"

"Put your contacts where your mouth is." She looked so defiant, she might have been challenging me to a duel instead of asking a favor. "You want to help battered women? Here's your chance. Come over to the house tonight and talk to her about it." And then, as if she were dragging the words over gravel, and it hurt, she added, "I'd appreciate it, Cain."

"Sure," I said.

I can never refuse a gracious request.

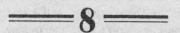

8

IT WAS THE BLOND TEENAGER WITH THE BLUE-EYED BABY named Shawnie. Her name was Marsha McEachen, her husband's name was Ernie. They were both nineteen years old, unemployed, married since they were fifteen, already the parents of two children. It seemed they had only recently started down the road of family violence.

"He only hit me that one other time before," Marsha whispered. She, Smithy, and I were cramped into the shelter's office early that evening. The soft, shy whisper continued: "It was just like last time, I was so surprised, all I could do was cry. And then Ernie cried, too, just like last time. And this time he promised me, he swore he'd never do it again."

"They always promise," Smithy said, but gently, as if she were breaking bad news. I had never heard that note of tenderness in Smithy's voice before. She directed her next words to me as if we two were adults in the presence of a child before whom one must speak in simple words and careful sentences. "Marsha wants to go back home tomorrow, Jenny. Her husband has agreed to go for counseling, so we'll hope for the best. Why don't you tell Jenny what started it this time, Marsha?"

The girl made a steeple of her hands and brought them to her mouth. Behind them, she said, "Every year we have the folks over to Thanksgiving, and I said we can't do it this time 'cause we don't have the money. And he said, was I blaming him for it. And I said, oh, no, it wasn't his fault. But then he started yelling about how we'd have more money if I didn't spend so much, but that's not true, honest, I hardly spend enough to feed the kids anymore, and then he really started yelling how I was blaming him for everything, and it wasn't his fault he lost his job, it was all because they gave his job to this black guy who wasn't half as good. And I asked him to kind of quiet down, because of the kids, you know? I didn't want to upset them. And he said . . ."

Behind her fingertips, her lips quivered.

"He said . . . I can't tell you what he said."

Tears began to roll down her plump cheeks.

"Is that when he hit you?" Smithy prompted her.

Marsha nodded dumbly.

"How many times?"

The girl swallowed noisily and her nose began to run. I jerked several tissues out of a box on Smithy's desk and gave them to her. Her fingertips, when we touched, were cold and damp.

"How many times, Marsha?" Smithy insisted.

"I don't know," she said into the tissues. "A lot. It

hurt a lot, and I was so scared, oh, God, I was so scared. And the kids were hollering, and, oh, God, it was awful. I was so ashamed, and I didn't ever want anybody to know, but even when Ernie started to cry and say he was sorry, I was still really scared, you know? And that's when I ran out with the kids and got in the car. And we went to this friend's house, but we couldn't stay there 'cause her husband knows my husband. So she had me call you, and now I know Ernie's really upset, and maybe I shouldn't have come here, I mean, he probably won't ever do it again, but I panicked, and it's all my fault.''

She had her eyes lowered, and for that reason she did not see, as I did, Smithy's lips pull back from her teeth in a silent snarl at those words.

"If I hadn't complained about Thanksgiving, it wouldn't have happened. If I'd just been more understanding . . .''

"You haven't done anything wrong!" Smithy fairly snapped it at the girl, so that Marsha's head jerked up and she stared at the older woman fearfully. "Remember that! You didn't hit him. He hit you. There is no excuse—ever—for him to hit you. You didn't do anything wrong, Marsha McEachen!''

Cowed, if not convinced, the girl nodded repeatedly.

"Marsha," I said, "would it help if he had a job?''

Her head reversed its motion, to nod vigorously. "Oh, yes!''

"What does he do?''

"Anything!" She blushed, brushed the tissue across her lips. "Factory work, sales, construction—Ernie can do most anything, and he's a real hard worker, Ms. Cain, you won't be sorry if you hire Ernie.''

"No, I can't hire him," I said, and then added quickly to ease the disappointment in her face, "but I'll try to find an employer who will. Do you think your husband would talk to me about it?''

The hope in her blue eyes turned to unmistakable fear and doubt. She gnawed on the knuckles of her left hand a few moments before saying, ''I think so, if he's still speaking to me.''

''What about you?'' I asked.

''Me?'' She pointed, like a child, at her chest.

''Do you want a job, too?''

''Oh.'' Marsha McEachen's eyes widened and, at last, she smiled. She looked even more like a child, one who's just been offered a banana split. ''That would be heaven!'' But then her smile drooped. ''But the kids—what would I do about my kids?''

''We'll see.'' Out of her sight, for the second time that day I crossed my fingers for luck. ''I'd like to get started on this. Would you call him now, Marsha, and find out if he'll see me tonight?''

She eagerly reached for the phone as if she couldn't wait to talk to him. But when Smithy and I rose to leave, to give her privacy, she grabbed my hand and tugged me back into my chair, and turned a pleading face toward Smithy, as well. We remained, fidgeting uncomfortably through the girl's emotional conversation with her husband.

''Ernie?'' she said in a breathless, trembling voice. ''I love you!''

I tried not to listen, focusing instead on the handwritten list of ''House Rules'' posted behind Smithy's desk. There were only four of them:

1. Don't tell anybody the location or address of this house, not even your mother.

2. No booze or drugs.

3. No violence, including verbal abuse.

4. No weapons.

Scrawled across the bottom was a warning—*"This is for your own safety!"* If a woman broke a rule, the sign said, she would be asked to leave immediately, and she would never be allowed to return to Sunrise House.

It was clear, from the end of the conversation I was trying not to overhear, that young Ernie McEachen was as anxious to reconcile with his wife as she was to see him again. It sounded, from her responses to him, as if he was frightened of what he had done, and deeply apologetic, and desperate to get his little family back.

"They're always so sorry," Smithy remarked to me, none too quietly.

He agreed to see me that night.

"See you tomorrow, honey!" Marsha cooed, and hung up.

"I'm so happy!" she exclaimed to us. "Thanks a lot for everything."

Marsha left us then, to check on her children.

When Smithy and I were alone in her office, she said, "Why can't you just talk to him over the phone, why do you want to meet him?"

"I'm not going to play personnel manager for a man I've never met."

"All right, but you'd better take Tommy Nichol with you."

"Tommy? Why, for heaven's sake?"

"Because McEachen probably won't talk to you if you take a cop along, which I'd sure as hell prefer you did."

She leaned toward me, looking intense. "You can't trust these guys, Cain, not for a minute. A man like Ernie McEachen, he's got a hot temper, he's unpredictable, and he's already proved he's violent. And usually, these guys want to blame anybody but themselves for their troubles. Besides, you don't know if he's sober. Tommy deals with these jerks all the time, so you'd better take Tommy along, just in case you need him."

I didn't see how cherubic Tommy Nichol could make a difference in a tight spot, but I called him anyway to appease Smithy. When she was assured he would meet me, she accompanied me to the front door of the shelter. On the way out, I glimpsed Eleanor Hanks and Mrs. Gleason in the dining room, feeding dinner to assorted youngsters.

"She's still here?" I said quietly to Smithy.

"Eleanor?" She looked back over her shoulder, then at me. "If you were her, would *you* want to go back to that house?"

"What's she going to do?"

"That," Smithy snapped, our momentary rapport quickly evaporating, "is up to your boyfriend, Cain. How long's he going to keep her in suspended animation? Are they going to arrest her or not? Eleanor didn't do it, Cain, any fool who meets her for one second can see that. It's cruel to keep her swinging in the wind like this."

"I don't think he's doing it on purpose, Smithy."

She looked at me pityingly. "Think again, Cain."

I stepped out of the house, giving her the chance to slam the door behind me. I heard the bolts shoot home.

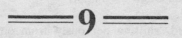

9

TOMMY NICHOL MET ME OUTSIDE THE McEACHENS'
address, which was a massive old Victorian house that
had been converted, probably illegally, into apartments.
To the white shirt and beige trousers he had added a yellow
windbreaker jacket, so now he looked like vanilla ice
cream dipped in butterscotch.

"Hi, Jenny!"

Tommy had his hands in the pockets of his jacket, and
he was bouncing on the balls of his feet. His big, eager
smile was the happy face on top of the cone.

Inwardly, I shook my head. "Hello, Tommy."

"Gosh, I hope we can do some good here!"

He looked as if he would melt like ice cream if a situation ever got hot. I couldn't imagine how he ever got his

clients to take him seriously, and I was beginning to regret Smithy's advice.

Nevertheless, I said, "Everest awaits."

The McEachens were four floors up, with no elevator. I had to pause on the second and third landings to let Tommy catch his breath. When I knocked at the Mc-Eachens' door, a slight, bearded blond youth opened it immediately, as if he had been standing with his ear to it, listening to us climb the stairs.

"Ernie?"

He nodded, shifting nervously from one foot to the other.

"I'm Jenny Cain, this is Tommy Nichol. May we come in?"

He squinted at us as if he had a headache. On closer inspection, I saw that the scraggly beard was probably intended to cover a bad complexion. He was skinny, pale, and as runty as an ill-fed boy. He said, "Yeah," and stood aside to admit us into the tiny living room. Once we were all in, though, he suddenly seemed to see his apartment through strangers' eyes—he began to race around like a jerky puppet, picking up magazines and dirty clothes. He tossed them into a bedroom and slammed the door on that mess. He carried dirty cups and dishes into the kitchenette and emptied ashtrays into a small metal wastebasket, missing the mark a bit, so that ashes drifted slowly to the stained carpet.

Tommy and I stood in the middle of the living room, glancing at each other, waiting for the tornado of activity to subside. Finally, Ernie McEachen wiped his hands on the front of his trouser legs.

"Excuse the mess, all right?" A nervous grin flickered, then disappeared from his thin face. "I guess I better get this place cleaned up before Marsha and the kids get home,

I mean, she'd be embarrassed if she knew you saw it looking like this. But with her gone, I just . . ."

Ernie stopped in his tracks then and stared at the floor as if overcome by the enormity of everything that had transpired. For an awful moment, I thought he was going to start sobbing. I wasn't so sure I could manage a sympathetic shoulder for him: "Gee, Ernie, I sure feel sorry for you that you beat your wife." I hoped I would not have to play psychologist that night, a role for which I was not trained or suited by nature. Tommy, who was trained, offered no assistance but merely sat down in a yellow director's chair, looking flushed.

The young husband pulled himself together and sat down in the far corner of his sofa. He leaned back and crossed his arms over his thin chest.

"I don't know what anybody told you," he said, his tone mingling defensive and belligerent notes, "but I love my wife and kids."

"Then why'd you hit her?"

Ernie and I both looked over, surprised, at Tommy.

"Hell, I didn't mean to!" Ernie said, looking sincere.

"You mean you didn't know what you were doing?"

"Yeah, right."

"Why?"

"Why?" Ernie looked at me as if I could explain this odd, pestering fat fly that had taken to buzzing around him.

"I mean," Tommy persisted calmly, "were you drunk?"

"No, I wasn't drunk!"

"High on anything else?"

"No, man!"

"Were you unconscious, had she knocked you out?"

"What the hell are you talking about anyway?" Again, his glance appealed to me for relief.

"Well, if you weren't drunk," Tommy said, "and you weren't high, and you weren't unconscious, did you know you were raising your hand to her?"

"What? Yeah, well, I knew it, but—"

"Did you know it was going to strike her face?"

"Well, God—"

"Did you?"

"I guess, but—"

"Did you?"

"Yes!"

"Then," Tommy said in his friendly voice, "I guess you meant to hit her, didn't you?"

"Jesus!" Ernie McEachen slouched farther into his corner. "Who are you, some fucking social worker? I didn't ask for no fucking social worker!"

"You agreed to counseling," Tommy said.

"I didn't agree to you," Ernie shot back.

"Well, I'm the counselor."

"Shit." Ernie turned his glare my way.

Tommy beamed his happy smile at me and nodded, as if granting permission for me to speak.

"Uh," I began, "Ernie, I'm here to help you find work."

He twisted around on the couch until he managed to put his back to Tommy. "Why? What's it to you?"

"I have contacts among employers." It was an answer that wasn't an answer. "If you'll tell me your qualifications, I might be able to get you some interviews. What can you do, Ernie?"

He looked scornful. "Twice as much as some of them management types sitting on their fat asses in their fancy offices, that's for sure."

"Maybe you could be more specific," I suggested.

He shrugged. "I could handle the line at the fish cannery, all right, probably be a supervisor in a couple of months. Yeah, it'd be okay if you'd get me on at the cannery."

Port Frederick Fisheries was our town's major employer. A Foundation trustee was the retired president of the company. "I can't promise you a job there, Ernie, because it will be up to you to impress them enough to win it for yourself." I could hear my caution making me pompous. "But, yes, I think I can get you an interview and put in a good word for you. I'll be happy to do that much."

Ernie McEachen rubbed his hands together fast and hard, as if they were flint and he were trying to start a spark of hope. But this business of finding him a job was the comparatively easy part; the hard part would come later when . . . if . . . he tried to change the attitudes and break the patterns of behavior that lifted his thin hands to strike her soft cheeks.

As if he were on my same wavelength, Tommy said, "We have a group that meets on Monday and Wednesday nights, Ernie."

"What kind of group?" Ernie crossed his arms defensively over his chest again and stared suspiciously at his tormentor.

"A good group." Tommy put his hands on his knees to push himself up out of the chair. "A group of men who want to stop hitting the women they love. You think you'd like to pay us a visit this Wednesday night, Ernie?"

"No, I wouldn't like to," he sneered. "Do I have a choice?"

Tommy smiled happily upon him. "There's always a choice, Ernie. That's what it's all about, making different choices. Anyway, you promised Marsha, didn't you?'' He handed Ernie his card.

The young husband nodded reluctantly, keeping his head down. But he took the card.

We were letting ourselves out of the McEachens' apartment when Ernie called out, ''Hey, I've got to pick up Marsha and the kids at that shelter place tomorrow, Sunset Shack, or whatever it is. Where is it anyway? She told me the address, but I forgot.''

He was squinting again, but this time it gave him a sly look.

''I don't know,'' Tommy said pleasantly. ''I've never been there myself.''

Ernie McEachen looked as if he didn't believe that, but rather than challenge his tormentor, he looked at me for the answer.

''Don't ask me,'' I said ambiguously, and shrugged.

Tommy and I completed our exit quickly.

On our way back down the four flights of stairs, Tommy whispered urgently to the back of my head, ''He'll keep after her until she tells him where it is. They always want to know, they *always* want to know where she went, it just *kills* them to think their women can hide someplace they can't find them. It's like a direct blow to the ego, you know, Jenny? It gives the women a little power they never had before, and the men *hate* it. A lot of times, the way they react is, they sell the second car, or they take the woman's keys away, or he tells her he'll beat her up if she ever leaves the house without his permission again. It's incredible how threatened they feel, you wouldn't believe it, Jenny! But you also wouldn't believe how the women break down and tell them what they want to know, where the shelter is, I mean. They want to get the old man off their case, and they think, the women think, what's the harm? But then it's a mess the next time they need help. Smithy can't take them then, she has to find them another safe house, and it's not that easy."

I reached the front door first and held it open for him.

"So it's dangerous for the men to find out," I said, to give him time to catch his breath. He was huffing from the exertion of talking and walking at the same time. I closed the door and joined him on the front walk.

"You said it," he continued breathlessly. "Jenny, I've heard of cases where the men have shown up on the doorstep with guns and shot up the place, trying to get to their wives. You just can't take any chances with it, you know?"

"I'm convinced."

Tommy suddenly flushed, and his next glance at me was shy. "I guess you probably think I was pretty hard on him."

"Well, he was pretty hard on her."

We started walking to our cars.

"Tommy," I said on impulse, and in recognition of the new respect I felt for his professional abilities, "while the doctor's in his office, let me ask you if you have any free advice for a cop who's feeling burned out?"

"Gosh, I don't believe there's any such thing as free advice."

"Nevertheless."

He gazed down at his own pigeon-toed stride for a moment, then looked back up and smiled at me. "Some studies indicate that a lot of people who go into social work—and that might include some cops—come from troubled homes themselves, Jenny. Supposedly, they choose their line of work because they still want to 'fix' their families, and if they can't manage that, they'll try to fix the world. Eventually, they see it can't be done, and that's when they get disillusioned and quit. Does any of that description fit your particular cop?''

''I'll have to think about it.''

He beamed at me. ''Well, 'bye, Jenny.''

I wondered if that description might fit a certain eager young psychologist who had not only failed to melt but had turned up the heat himself. Behind that happy face, he seemed to be full of surprises—and a troubled family history would only be one more. Gazing at Tommy's back as he trotted off to his car, I noticed for the first time that in order to be shaped like an ice-cream cone, a man had to have pretty broad shoulders.

''Good night, Tommy.''

Having done my good deed for the day, I went home.

10

I SHOULD HAVE KNOWN IT COULDN'T BE THAT EASY TO win a merit badge. By the middle of the week, my foray into the world of social services threatened to swamp my time, what with the members of the new task force calling repeatedly to report on their progress with the committee's ideas.

"I've set up a meeting with the Board of Education," Sabrina announced when she called.

"Great," I said.

"They seem pretty interested," she continued, "as long as we don't offend any right-wing conservative groups who believe in a man's God-given right to beat the shit out of his wife and kids. Personally, I can't think of any groups I'd rather offend, can you?"

"Not offhand," I said.

Then Kathy Ingram called to suggest a name for the coalition.

"I thought of SAVE, for Stand Against Violent Encounters," she said in her soft, precise voice, "but Henry says that implies a certain violence itself, so I thought of SAFE—for Spouses Against Family Enmity—but that's rather negative, and it does exclude the unmarried, so I thought maybe we'd do a survey."

"SAFE sounds great," I said quickly, making a stand against expensive and time-consuming statistical encounters (SATE). "It doesn't have to be an acronym, after all. SAFE is short, it's meaningful and appropriate, and I hereby declare it the official name of the coalition."

"Don't you think we ought to call a meeting and take a vote?"

"No," I said firmly.

"Cain," Smithy said when her turn came, "I've been thinking about the crisis hotline, and I think our volunteers could handle it."

"Sounds good," I said, while thinking that I had certainly put together an odd sort of coalition to work on saving families—five single people out of eight, and only one parent among the lot of us. I wondered if maybe later I should add some other married folks and parents to this task force.

By Thursday morning, I had managed to think of two people I knew who were happily married, and was trying to come up with a third name when Tommy Nichol called.

"What about the police?" he inquired. "If they want that special training course, I could handle the section on dealing with perpetrators."

"I haven't heard from the police on that yet," I admitted with regret. "But speaking of your counseling sessions, did Ernie McEachen show up last night?"

"Yes." Tommy chuckled; it was a merry sound that seemed weirdly at odds with his subject, but then, I supposed, in his line of work it paid to take the long view, and long views tend to contain some humor. "The other guys really let him have it when he got defensive, and that shocked him. He thought the other men would be on his side, but most of them are only on their own side. They can see his faults all right, just not their own." He chuckled. "I'd say we're still in the 'poor me' stage with Ernie."

"What comes next?"

He chuckled again, a mannerism I was finding vaguely annoying. "The pissed-off stage, I call it, Jenny," he said. "That's where he's mad at them, and me, and Marsha, and God, and his parents, and every third person he ever knew."

"And then?"

This time he didn't laugh. "Then? Well, maybe a little grief, a little regret, a few apologies. And then, in that very brief moment when he's seeing himself for who he really is, then we start to work. If we're lucky, he decides he wants to change, and that makes all the difference."

"How often do you get lucky, Tommy?"

"Not often," he admitted cheerfully. I was changing my mind about Tommy again; he didn't remind me so much of an ice-cream cone anymore as he did of a buoyant little boat, improbably bobbing on rough seas. Did he ever feel swamped? I wondered. He was saying, "But I have a feeling about Ernie."

"A hopeful feeling?"

"Yes! If I can just get him past all his anger and resentment . . ."

"That's a big if."

Tommy sighed, though he didn't sound in the least discouraged. "You said it!"

"Is Marsha in any danger from him now, Tommy?"

"She will always be in danger, Jenny," he replied, a shade dramatically, "unless the tiger changes his stripes."

That seemed even more unlikely with the next call, which came from Ernie McEachen himself. He told me that he got the interview at Port Frederick Fisheries, but not the job.

"You *told* me," he said accusingly. "You said—"

"I said I'd get you the interview, and the rest was up to you, Ernie. What happened?"

"They said they wanted somebody with experience." He laughed bitterly. "How am I supposed to get the experience if I can't get the job. You *told* me—"

"I didn't promise a job."

"Yeah, but . . ."

"I didn't promise anything but an interview. Did I?"

Silence, then a grudging, "I guess not. But what do I do now?"

"Is Marsha home yet?"

"Yeah." He sounded happier. "It's really great now. Or it was going to be great, until they didn't give me the job. I don't know what I'm going to do now."

The whining note in his voice made me turn brisk, verging on brusque. "Let's back up a step, Ernie. Tell me again, what jobs do you have experience at?"

"I don't know," he said listlessly.

"Name two."

"Well, I don't know, the last job I had, I sold magazines over the phone, and I've had a couple jobs in filling stations, pumping gas, you know, but they don't pay nothin'."

"They must pay something, Ernie."

"With two kids?" He sounded indignant now.

"Okay, I'll see if I can get you a few more interviews. But Ernie, you can't depend on this, you understand? You've got to try on your own, get down to the employment office, check the want ads, maybe put in an ad yourself for position wanted. I'll help if I can, but that's all."

"Right," he said, more agreeably this time. But then he added, as if I had not uttered any caveats, "See if you can get me something around seven bucks an hour, all right?"

"Oh, Ernie," I said, and sighed to myself. In addition to his employment problems, I had offered to see about getting work for his wife, not to mention child care. So when I hung up from talking to him, I put in a call to one of our town's other major employers.

"Lars," I said to my brother-in-law, "it's Jennifer."

"Here comes the bride," he sang in a jovial bass. My brother-in-law, Lars Guthrie, was a man of simple needs: money, a beautiful wife, an immaculate home, obedient children, membership in a good country club, handball twice a week, and a spot on the board of his Episcopal church. Fortunately, a sweet nature and a juvenile sense of humor saved him from impossible stuffiness. "It's going to be a bang-up party, Jennifer. Sherry's really breaking her back to make it nice for her big sister." Wryly, he added, "Not to mention breaking the budget."

"Budget? Sherry and budget? Now, Lars, you know those are mutually exclusive terms."

He laughed in the manner of a true but tried husband. To ease the sting, I lied, "But it's nice of you, and I'm grateful. And I'll be even more grateful if you do me another favor, Lars. Two, really. I know a young couple who are unemployed and who desperately need help. She could probably do light clerical work, and he could handle manual labor. Do you have any openings?''

Lars Guthrie owned and managed Lars Brand Labels, the only discount clothing store in Port Frederick, the one whose $29.95 dresses put $299.95 dresses on my sister's back.

''You think she could do part-time sales, Jenny?''

''I think she'd jump at it.''

''Great. I like my employees to jump at my beck and call.'' His chuckle came over the phone as an infectious rumble. ''Send her in, Jenny. We're about to lay off a couple of our full-time saleswomen, and I'm hoping we can take up the slack with somebody who's only part-time. I'll tell my personnel manager to expect her, what's her name?''

''Marsha McEachen. What about him, Lars?''

''The husband? Can't help you there, sorry.''

''You're a peach, Lars.''

''Get to the party early, then, before I start fermenting.''

He was still laughing at his own rotten pun when we hung up. I added the Guthries to my list of ''happily marrieds''; maybe I couldn't have lived with her, but Lars seemed contented enough, and I suspected Sherry, in her own weird way, was, too.

Talking about employment and thinking about marriage made me think suddenly of Willie's wife, Gail Henderson, who had also said she needed a job, now that they had moved away from the better-paying cop jobs of Boston. I started to call Lars back to inquire about other part-time openings, but then thought better of getting involved in yet another family's private business. I wasn't an employment agency, after all. Maybe I'd call Gail later, from home, and see whether she even *wanted* any help from me.

Well, I thought then, maybe I had solved one of the McEachens' problems. Or made it worse? How would a man like Ernie McEachen take it if his wife got a job, and he did not? I sighed again and called them back to find out.

But Ernie was not home when I reached Marsha.

"Oh, thank you!" she gushed when I told her.

"What about the children?"

"I guess Ernie could watch them until he finds a job," she replied, although she sounded doubtful about it. I wasn't too crazy, myself, about the idea of their violent father caring for them alone. Without telling her the reason behind my concern, I promised to help her find other arrangements. Then I wished her good luck, hung up, and began to call all over town, trying to trade in my chips for interviews for her husband. Everyone I talked to was sympathetic, but nobody had anything to offer. Finally, I played the last ace.

"Detective Bushfield," he answered the phone.

The sound of his voice triggered an unbusinesslike current of desire through my body. As usually happened when he had a major case to solve, we had not been seeing much of each other; the very male sound of his voice reminded me that I missed him, and in what specific ways.

"Geof, I know you don't like to get involved in your family's business, but I need a favor." His family owned Bushware, Inc., one of the largest hardware and plumbing supply companies in the Northeast. Although the rest of the family and the company headquarters were located out of state, there were branch stores in our area. "Would you call around and see if any of the stores needs a salesman, or somebody for manual labor?"

"I thought you loved your job."

I laughed. "This is for the husband of a woman at Sunrise House."

"Who, Jenny?" He sounded distracted, as if he were reading reports while he talked to me.

"Ernie McEachen's his name."

"McEachen." Now he sounded more alert, as if he had put down the reports to concentrate on putting a face to the name. "Wait a minute. Scrawny little guy with a short fuse and bad skin? Lives in a converted Victorian with a pudgy wife and a couple of kids?"

"That's the one."

In the background, I heard the loud creak that his swivel chair emitted when he leaned back in it. "He's a nasty piece of work, Jenny. If you'd seen what he did to his wife a couple of months ago, I don't think you'd want to be doing him any favors."

"I'm not doing it for him. Besides, she thinks that will stop if he gets a job."

"That's what they all say."

"You sound like Smithy Leigh."

He laughed. "You could accuse me of worse things, but at the moment I can't think what they could be. Don't you ever wonder why Smithy hates men so much? I mean, I'll grant you she sees the species at our worst, but hell, I've seen a truckload of worthless women in my job, and I don't hate the rest of you." The chair creaked again, as if he had sat up straight once more. Before I could reply to what was evidently only a rhetorical question, he said, "Well, all right, I'll call the area manager and pull rank for you. But you'd better understand that I'm going to tell him the truth about Ernie McEachen, Jenny."

"But tell him that Ernie needs one more chance, too."

"I'll tell him you told me to say that."

"All right!" I smiled at the phone. "It's all I ask."

"Why are you getting involved with them, Jenny?"

"Actually, I'm trying pretty hard *not* to get any more involved with them. It's just a favor for Sunrise House, that's all. Smithy challenged me to put my business connections where my mouth is and help out one of her battered women. What's new on the Hanks case, Geof?"

"Still no confession." He sounded discouraged, a bad sign, since it was still fairly early in the investigation. "No witnesses, no direct evidence. And no other suspects, either."

"Geof, would you mind if I talked to her again?"

"To Mrs. Hanks? Why?"

"For our task force."

"Your task force."

"Whatever. I was thinking we ought to have a victim advocate, and while it probably wouldn't be Eleanor Hanks, I'd still like to talk to her."

"Same question: why?"

"I want to ask her, from the perspective of her own experience, how she thinks we might help other families."

He was quiet for a moment, obviously thinking it over. "I don't know, I guess it can't hurt. Sure, talk to her. But stay off the subject of murder, Jenny, so we don't run into legal problems if there turns out to be a case against her."

"I do so solemnly swear."

"That's the way—practice those vows."

"Oil that chair," I retorted.

I hung up thinking that he was a fine one to talk about vows, having sworn twice before to "take this woman for as long as you both shall live." Maybe that was an unreasonable expectation? Or maybe, with all that practice, he'd get it right this time.

* * *

I called Sunrise House to make an appointment with Eleanor Hanks. As I waited for someone to answer the phone at the shelter, I gazed longingly at the piles of work on my desk and hoped she would agree to an evening appointment.

"555-7532."

"Hello. May I speak to Mrs. Hanks?"

"This is an answering service," a female voice replied. "I don't know if there is a Mrs. Hanks residing at the number you called, but I will be glad to take your name and phone number so that she can call you back, if there's anyone there by that name."

I had forgotten: They never divulged the identities of women at the house. The business about the answering service was, in fact, a lie designed for confidentiality and security.

I left my number. Eleanor Hanks called back within five minutes.

I explained to her, vaguely, that I was heading a task force dealing with families. "And as part of our research, I'd like to get the opinions of women who have been residents of shelters like Sunrise House. May I come over and talk to you sometime soon?"

"Well, normally, I'd be at work, but I haven't gone back. Uh, I've just put the baby down for a nap." She sounded tired and distracted, but pleasant. "And the other two kids are at school, so this would be about the only free time I'd have. Could you come over now?"

"Sure." I averted my glance from the piles of work on my desk. "I'll be right there."

=====11=====

As I parked at Sunrise House, a fat black woman in a yellow print tent dress—Mrs. Gleason—was loading five children into a station wagon. An elderly white woman, most likely one of the volunteers, was the driver. After she got the children in, Mrs. Gleason crammed a battered suitcase into the back of the wagon, and then maneuvered her own bulk into the front seat. If I had been closer, I imagine I might have heard her grunt. She might have been only twenty-five years old as Geof had said, but she moved like a sixty-year-old charwoman.

I reached the front door as they drove off, the children looking still and serious in the rear of the wagon. Their mother propped her vast, pendulous right arm on the rim of the open window on the passenger's side, and faced straight ahead. She didn't look back, but the children did. One of them waved.

Smithy, who was standing in the doorway, waved back.

"She's going back to him again."

"Why?"

"For the children, she says." Smithy's voice was bitter, ironic. "And because her preacher says it's her duty."

"What do you say?"

Her eyes narrowed as the station wagon turned left at the corner. I thought suddenly of the stone house waiting to take them in again, and I wondered if the malevolent fat man was still sitting on the stoop, hungry for the final feast. I shook away the image as Smithy replied, "I say the husband should drop dead along with the preacher, but dead is too good for either of them." With a jerk of her head, she invited me into the shelter. I felt strongly the aptness of the word. Shelter.

"Eleanor's waiting for you. Is this for the task force?"

"Yes." I stepped in, leaving her outside.

"You should have checked it out with me, Cain."

"She's a grown woman." I fought my annoyance. "She can make her own decisions."

"They haven't done her much good so far."

Annoyance won. "Why do you hate them all so much, Smithy?"

"Who? Men?"

I nodded.

"You would, too, if you saw what I see every day, Cain," she said condescendingly. "Like your boyfriend said, it's the result of accumulated evidence."

"I don't know," I said, feeling goaded. "People accumulate evidence to support the opinions they want to prove. Maybe you've just managed to find a line of work that allows you to rationalize your feelings."

She didn't reply.

"A person could accumulate evidence to prove the opposite," I insisted, although I was already regretting that I'd let her prick me into striking back. "And you could start by collecting the names of men like Geof Bushfield, Tommy Nichol—"

"You think Tommy's different?" She looked at me and laughed; it was the cold, victorious laugh of the fighter who has just seen the light between your glove and your jaw. "He's just as violent as the rest of them. You ask sweet little Tommy sometime about how he decked Lanny Gleason's husband one time when he got out of line at one of those counseling sessions."

"But that's—"

"Different? Men are violent, Cain. Period."

I wasn't going to win this one, so I stopped trying. I didn't want to leave any more animosity between us than there usually was, however, so I tried for a moment's bland conversation.

"Okay." I smiled at her. "I bow to your greater experience. Although I don't know what it is. What *did* you do before you came here, Smithy?"

"I was in school," she said, calmer now that she'd won. "Getting my degree in social work. And I was working part-time at a shelter."

"Where?"

"Boston."

"That's where you're from, Smithy?"

"Yeah." She shrugged, then said, as if admitting to something that embarrassed her, "Back Bay."

It didn't surprise me; Smithy so determinedly cultivated a working-class image that it practically had to hide middle- or upper-class origins. "Your family still there?"

Her head snapped around, and she glared at me as if

my bland question had mortally insulted her. "What is this, amateur psychology hour? You're a great one to talk about crazy parents, Cain."

"Huh? Where did *that* come from? What the hell is that supposed to mean, Smithy?" Actually, I knew exactly what it was supposed to mean, and I was furious. "Listen, my father never abused my mother," I said hotly, wishing I didn't sound so defensive. Even as I defended him, I thought: it was true, he'd never hit her, only neglected and deserted her. Only. But no, I couldn't stand to think of him as abusive, only selfish and unaware as a child might be.

Tears sprang to her eyes. "Lucky you."

The argument was over. She closed the door between us.

I stared at the door for a few moments, feeling as if I'd just stepped in from a sudden violent squall. Jesus, the woman was touchy! But then I felt myself smiling at the door. Look who's talking. I breathed deeply a couple of times and turned around.

The place was dim and silent, the curtains drawn.

I suddenly felt claustrophobic and wanted back out again. It was hard to breathe in the air that seemed thick with tears, fear, unhappiness, and anger. When I found Eleanor Hanks sitting with her hands folded in her lap in the living room, I suggested we go someplace else to talk.

"Where?" she asked, as if, having lived there for a few days, she was now bewildered and a little terrified by the idea of a world outside of Sunrise House.

"What's in the backyard?"

"A sandbox." She looked doubtful. "Swings."

"That'll do." I coaxed her into getting her coat from upstairs, then led her to the back door, where I had to unhook a chain, draw a bolt, and turn a key in a lock in order to go outside. The security around this place was no small inconvenience and no joke. "Wait," she said softly, and left me standing alone in the kitchen. In a moment she was back with another woman who locked the door behind us.

"They get really upset if somebody leaves a door open, even back here," Eleanor explained. "We can knock when we want somebody to let us in."

We walked down the steps, but not into the airy, open space I craved. The backyard was like another locked room. True, this one had sky for a ceiling and grass for a rug. But it was surrounded by an eight-foot fence that was constructed of pointed, wooden slats that were nailed tightly together so that nobody could see in. Or out. The only view was up at the chilly blue sky. There were two gates, both strongly barred. It only lacked a moat to complete the feeling of being in a fortress.

Still, it was better than staying in the house.

"Let's sit there," I said, and pointed to a children's playground set. It was metal, painted white with red stripes, with a slide, rings, and one of those swings with facing benches. We climbed awkwardly into the double swing and sat down on opposite sides, our hands wrapped around the metal supports, our thighs touching. My knees rubbed the front of the bench where she sat. She was shorter; her knees didn't touch the metal. I pressed the toe of my right shoe to the ground and pushed, to start us swinging.

She had been glancing at me and looking increasingly upset.

"I remember you." She moved her leg away from mine so they no longer touched. Her face looked pinched, and she seemed to shrink into her thin coat, as if she were cold. "You were here with those detectives. You're a policewoman, aren't you?"

"No, nothing like that."

But she still had a suspicious, betrayed look in her eyes.

"Smithy will tell you," I assured her. I hated to admit it, but Smithy was right—I should have gone through channels to get to this frightened woman. "She and I are both members of a task force that is looking into the problem of family violence in Port Frederick. We'd like to find ways to help other families avoid some of the troubles you've had, Mrs. Hanks." She didn't suggest that I call her Eleanor. I could hear myself going stiff and awkward in the face of her dismay. "I thought that one of the best ways to start was to talk to women who've been there, in violent family situations, that is." She was frowning now, as if she were trying to understand what I was saying, but at the same time she was shaking her head vigorously, as if she were going to refuse to answer me. I figured it was my own fault that I'd lost her, and I braced myself to be turned down. Sounding more like a bureaucrat every second, I said, "I don't want to intrude on your privacy. But if you're willing to discuss it with me, I'd like to ask you what you think might be some of the causes of family violence, and what you think our community might do to help prevent—"

"But it wasn't like that!" She made fists of her hands, and beat them on her lap. My foot slipped off the slats and struck the ground, causing the swing to jerk us. "I don't know why nobody ever believes me, but it wasn't like that at all! Dick was a wonderful husband, really he was, and he never hit me, not once! My goodness, that would have been mortifying to him, in his position. Oh, we had our arguments, like any married couple, but it was never like that, never! I feel embarrassed even to be here. . . ." She glanced at Sunrise House. "I wish somebody would believe me! I didn't kill him!"

"Mrs. Hanks, I don't think we ought to talk about—"

"I loved him! I wouldn't ever hurt him, any more than he'd ever hurt me! I don't understand why nobody believes me!"

How would Tommy Nichol handle this? I wondered.

"But Mrs. Hanks," I said, "weren't the police called to your home?"

She looked back toward the house. "Why, no."

"A couple of times this year, the neighbors called . . ."

"Oh, but that was a mistake." She stared at the empty half of the swing beside me. "The kids had the TV turned up real loud, and there was a movie on where a man and woman were shouting at each other, that's what the neighbors heard, it was all a mistake. We were so embarrassed, this whole thing is so mortifying, I could just die."

"Twice?"

"What?" She looked at me, then back at the house.

"The neighbors made the same mistake twice?"

"Yes, well, I don't know if it was the TV the second time, I don't remember exactly, but it was definitely all a mistake. Dick would tell you that, too." At the mention of her husband's name, she bit her lip and squinted as if to hold back tears. "He was a wonderful husband, we had a wonderful life together, and now . . ."

She bent her face into her hands and began to cry.

"I'm sorry." I wanted to ask her why, if it was such a great marriage, they had been interview subjects for the Ingrams, and why she had gone to the social welfare office to ask about assistance. But she was already down, and I couldn't bring myself to kick her again. "Do you want to go back in the house, Mrs. Hanks?"

She raised her face and stared at me, the tears streaming.

"I want to go back in time," she whispered. "Please, I just want to go back in time, and make it all go away."

In a few minutes, when she would allow me, I knocked on the door and guided her into Sunrise House. I handed her over to Smithy, who gave me a furious stare in return.

"You and Bushfield make a great pair, Cain," she said.

I didn't feel like arguing with her anymore.

On my way back to the office, I decided to stop by the single room that Dr. Henry and Kathy Ingram rented for their research. After parking on the street, I let myself in through the side door of the old, two-story brick building, climbed the dirty stairway, and knocked on the frosted-glass pane in the center of their unmarked, locked door. It didn't, as the Ingrams had commented on their application to the Foundation for funding, take much money to open research headquarters. It did require a fair amount to run their computer and buy their time. There were lights on within, so I knew somebody was there, because the Ingrams were sticklers for turning out lights and turning down heat, but for a few minutes, nobody answered my knock. If I knew Henry, he was in there, all right, keeping quiet, shushing Kathy, hoping the unexpected visitor would give up and go away. I knocked louder.

"Kathy? Henry?"

"What?" came a bad-tempered bellow from within.

"Jennifer Cain," I yelled back.

There was another long silence, then a voice said, "Hell's bells." Heavy footsteps approached the door, a bolt turned, and the door opened to reveal Henry in blue jeans and a black turtleneck sweater. He looked younger than his seventy-four years, but no more convivial than usual.

"Hello. We're busy." Henry turned around and plodded back to his desk, but he left the door open. I stepped into their office, which looked as clean, efficient, and modern as the rest of the building looked old, filthy, and messy. Henry, who was not entirely without courtesy, muttered loudly, "Come in."

"Hi, Henry, sorry to bother you. Where's Kathy?" I was hoping he would say she had just stepped out to pick up their usual working lunch from the nearby deli. But no such luck.

"Conducting interviews," he snapped. He began punching his long, meaty fingers onto the keyboard of one of his IBM computers, working busily as if I weren't there.

I was, by that time, becoming heartily tired—an interesting oxymoron—of rude people; it would have been a pleasure to see Kathy's warm, sweet smile, to be the recipient of her formal courtesy, to deal with her instead of him. The small room was nauseatingly full of his cigar smoke, which he was continuing to puff out at a rate approximating that of a good-size steam engine. I was going to have to make this a quick visit, or risk throwing up into their photocopying machine.

"Henry!" I said sharply.

He turned around then, peering at me through a thundercloud of black smoke. I moved fast, pulling up a chair beside him, and starting to talk rapidly—not so much to keep his attention as to get out of there as soon as possible.

"This won't take long, Henry," I promised. "I've just been to see Eleanor Hanks, who claims she didn't kill her husband. She claims they didn't argue, didn't fight, that Mr. Hanks never beat her up. And she's very convincing,

Henry. But what I wonder is, if that's true, why did you and Kathy interview the Hankses?''

He pursed his lips around the cigar and narrowed his eyes at me. Finally, about the time I thought I might pass out from oxygen depletion, he removed the cigar and stubbed it out in an ashtray on his desk. I would have breathed deeply with relief, but in that air, the act might have killed me.

''Can't tell you that,'' Henry said, mildly enough.

''Because it's confidential, I suppose?''

''Of course it is.'' He nodded. ''What kind of scientists would we be if we told all the dirty little secrets our subjects tell us? It would not only be unprofessional, it would be unethical, immoral, and inhumane.''

''Well, let me put it this way—''

''There is no way you can put it, Jennifer, that would loosen my tongue,'' he said sternly, but not unpleasantly. ''And don't go jumping to the conclusion that because we interviewed them, it must logically follow that theirs was a violent marriage.''

''But why would you interview them unless—''

''You've heard of control groups.'' It was a flat statement, not a question, and it gave me hope for Eleanor. Of course I'd heard of control groups.

''You mean you also interview nonviolent families, to contrast their behavior and attitudes with the violent ones?'' He nodded, but the fingers of his right hand were beginning to tap impatiently on his desk. I was afraid that any minute they'd move toward the ashtray and matches. ''So you're saying that you might have interviewed the Hankses as part of one of your control groups?''

He grabbed the cold, stubby cigar and just before sticking it back in his mouth, said, ''No, I am not saying that. I told you, I'm not saying anything.''

"You are a very difficult man, Henry," I informed him. He grinned around his cigar as he lit it.

"But apparently Kathy loves you," I conceded, getting up and backing rapidly away from him, "so you must have some redeeming features."

It amused him, as I knew it would. When I looked back at him just before I shut the door behind me, he was still smiling around his cigar.

I drove back to work then, feeling utterly confused and wondering how Geof ever solved anything, given that all he had to work with were unpredictable human beings! Besides, Eleanor Hanks and the good doctor had just shot to hell what little was left of my original fantasy of her husband's murder.

Or maybe they hadn't.

$$===== 12 =====$$

"SHE'S LYING, JENNY."

I met Geof for dinner that night. The restaurant, a chrome-and-linoleum joint named Johnnie's that seemed to change owners and names every three months, had the sole distinction of being close to the police station. It was also quick and cheap, although judging by the thickness of my pork tenderloin sandwich, not nearly cheap enough.

Geof's collar was open and his tie was undone, presenting to my view a triangle of skin and collarbone that I had kissed many times under many different circumstances. I was tempted even at that moment, but there was a table of greasy food between us.

"We were called to the house twice." He paused to wipe mayonnaise off his mouth. "I'm positive he'd beaten her both times. Now I'll grant you, there wasn't any blood, and she wasn't bruised anywhere I could see. And they both denied it. But I'll swear she moved as if she hurt, and she was afraid of him. That woman was scared to death the entire time we were there, both times.''

"Most people are nervous when cops come to call.'' I spouted his own wisdom back at him. "Even innocent people. Maybe she was scared for their reputation, how it would look to the neighbors.''

He gave me a look over his cheeseburger.

"But you didn't see any proof that he hit her,'' I pointed out.

"Jenny, there are so many ways to hit a person where it doesn't show.''

"I know that.'' I took a bite of my dinner, swallowed. When I didn't taste meat, I lifted a corner of the soggy bun to see if there really was any protein hiding there. Yes, there were two thin slices of dill pickle, a bit of onion, and just enough breaded pork to see with the naked eye. "But Geof . . .''

He pointed a French fry at me. "He'd been trained in security, remember, so he may have known how to punch her to produce maximum pain, minimum display.''

I put my sandwich back down on my plate. Every now and then I was brought up short by the cold, dark side of the reality of his occupation.

"I suppose you know how to do that, too.''

He nodded, his mouth full.

I let it go. "But you couldn't swear he hit her.''

He smiled slightly, shook his head. "Jenny, it's called denial. What she's doing, it's called denial.''

"Yes,'' I conceded, "I suppose it is.''

"Although, I'll admit she's pretty convincing.''

"Why, thank you.'' I laughed, and took up my tenderloin again. "So I'm not the only one who tends to believe her when she says she didn't do it."

"I didn't say I believe her, Jenny. But I will say that a lot of women lie about whether or not the old man beats them up, but that doesn't make them killers. Anyway, she hasn't confessed yet. That's suggestive. I know you won't like this, but most housewives are a snap to break down—they'll tell us the truth if we look at them cross-eyed."

"Oh, you chauvinistic cops are all alike." An image flitted through my mind: a line of tough-looking cops, arms akimbo, staring cross-eyed at a trembling housewife. "Besides, she manages that fast-food joint—or used to, anyway—so she isn't 'just' a housewife. She might be tougher than you think she is. I've known some housewives who were tougher than beef jerky."

He smiled slightly. "You should have been a lawyer—you'll take any side of an argument. The point is, hell, if she didn't kill him, maybe she's telling the truth about the other times. Maybe he never hit her, maybe the kids really did have the TV turned up too loud."

"The Ingrams used Eleanor and Dick as subjects for their research into domestic violence."

He looked interested. "I didn't know that."

"I asked Henry about it today, but he wouldn't tell me if that means they had a violent marriage; it might only mean they were part of a control group. But I do have this for you."

I thrust some stapled papers I had brought with me toward him. He took them, looking first quizzical, then appreciative. "How'd you get this, Jenny?"

It was a sample of the questionnaire the Ingrams used to interview their subjects. "I remembered it was part of their grant application, that's all."

He scanned the questions, running down them with his

right forefinger, reading a few aloud: "Frequency of arguments. Intensity of arguments. Causes of arguments. Episodes of physical violence, other than sexual. Episodes of rape, and other forcible sexual acts. Duration of violence. Has either partner ever pulled a gun against the other partner, or a knife? Damage resulting from violence. Medical records. How much he earns, how much she earns, how often they get a baby-sitter and go out together, activities independent of each other, attitudes, hobbies, church affiliations, other interests outside the home, extramarital affairs, substance dependency and abuse . . . Jesus, Jenny, this is a couple's life history, practically down to how often they pare their toenails. I thank you, ma'am."

"You're welcome. Do you think they'll talk to you?"

"The Ingrams? Well, if not to me, then maybe to a subpoena."

"What does Willie say now about the Hanks case?"

"Willie says she done him wrong." He laid down the questionnaire, took up his sandwich again. "But he doesn't have any evidence to prove it. What we need in this case is a big, fat break."

For some reason, that reminded me of my sister.

"Geof, are you going to be able to go to the party?"

"Party?" The way he said it, as if he were trying to remember the meaning of the word, didn't reassure me. "Oh, sure. One way or another. I promise."

"It's not me you'll have to answer to, it's Sherry."

He grimaced. "In that case, I swear it."

I didn't have the courage to ask the same question about our wedding. If he didn't get a break in the Hanks case soon, he just might say, no, sorry, he'd be working that night.

"Are the Hendersons going to the party?" I asked him.

"Gail and Willie? I don't know." He pulled out his

wallet, opened it, and shook his head. "Do you have any money, Jenny?"

"Haven't you and Willie talked about it?"

He looked surprised at the question. "The party? No."

I tried to imagine two women working together every day and never mentioning the party to which one of them was invited and for which the other was a guest of honor. I shook my head, too. My imagination was active, but not that active.

"What's the matter?" he asked. "Are we going to have to wash dishes?"

"Men," I remarked, "are different from women."

"Yeah, we usually carry more cash on us."

A black waitress in a pink uniform appeared. "Pie?"

"Is it fresh?" Geof inquired.

She shifted her weight to her other hip. "Do I have the right to remain silent?"

We laughed, and she slapped the check on our table.

"I'll get it," I said, and he started to get up from the table. I put out a hand to stop him. "Geof, I know you're in a hurry, but we really need to talk about the wedding."

"I'm leaving you with all the work, aren't I?" He sat down again, looking guilty and apologetic. "What's left to do?"

What *was* left to do? Pick up my dress from the seamstress, buy new shoes, get my hair done, check on the dinner reservations, pick up the airline tickets, take a shower, put on perfume, get him a boutonniere, pick up my own flowers. Most of that he couldn't do for me, and the rest I could manage on my own if I had to. So why had I even mentioned it? Because I wanted to know if our marriage still lurked somewhere in his mind, squeezed into his mental case files before "mayhem" and "murder." Or, a sardonic voice in my head suggested, because it lurked in my own head, along with "martyr" and "maybe."

"Get your suit pressed," I suggested.

"And show up?"

"That, too."

Again, he started to rise from the table.

"Geof . . ." I shot my next words out quickly, like darts, to pin him to the booth awhile longer. "Have you given any more thought to the idea about a special police training course in handling domestic disputes?"

"No."

"Are you going to?"

"What, think about it?" He sounded as if he were trying to curb annoyance with patience. "I don't know, it's hard to work up interest in something I may not be around to use."

My heart descended to my stomach, to mix with the greasy tenderloin and fries. "Then you're still thinking of quitting . . . that is, leaving . . . the force?"

"Well, not tonight, anyway." He made a visible effort to smile. "On this particular night, at this specific moment, I'm going back to work. See you later."

"All right."

He did get up from the table then, shrugged into his topcoat, bent down to kiss the top of my head, and left me to pay the bill. I stared at it for a while, thinking that cheap as it was, the price was still too high for so little sustenance. And what if I convinced him to change his mind about quitting? Then, someday, would I be making the same complaint about being a cop's spouse—too high a price to pay for too little sustenance? I walked to the counter and paid the cashier grudgingly.

I trudged to my car, feeling heavy and a little depressed,

as if an acute case of emotional indigestion was coming on.

On the way home I stopped by Gail Henderson's house.

"I'm sorry about the other night," I said, when she answered her doorbell. She was looking at me with a surprised and fixed smile on her thin face. "I tried to call." Lord, I thought, I sounded like some men I'd known. "Did you find the pizza before the kids stepped on it?"

"Yes." But her tone was cool, as if she didn't care much for sausage with extra cheese. Neither did she seem to care to invite me inside, but I was getting used to cool receptions. "Thank you."

"Well." I struggled for something to say. "Can you and Willie come to the party?"

"Oh, yes!" At last, there was inflection, even eagerness in her voice, and her face lit up. "Thank you so much for asking us, Jenny! I'm so excited about getting to go out somewhere! I'm practically all ready to go right now." She laughed, a real laugh this time, not a forced one. "I've got the baby-sitter lined up, and I've let the hem down on this really pretty dress I wore last year to a christening—I know the invitation said informal, but I hardly ever get a chance to dress up, so I hope nobody will mind if I wear a party dress—and I talked Willie into taking me out to dinner first, before the party! I just can't wait! It'll be so nice to meet people. I'm so grateful, it's just so thoughtful of you to ask us, Jenny!"

She was chattering like a teenager.

"Mom! Mommy, come here!"

She glanced behind her and seemed to find some minor disaster there. "Oh, God, sorry, Jenny." But this time, her voice was friendly, even though she still didn't ask me in. "Thanks for coming by. I'll see you Saturday night, all right?"

"Right, Gail."

With a quick smile, she closed the door.

I backed off the porch, a little shaken by the extreme fervor of her sociability. It implied the presence of its opposite—equally extreme loneliness.

When I got home, I made a call to try to staunch some of that loneliness that had gushed out of Gail Henderson like a hemorrhage.

"Sabrina?" I said, when she answered. After a few minutes of chitchat about the coalition, I said, "Remember that cop at the meeting? I think his wife, Gail, is pretty lonely, being new in town. I'd like to get the two of you together for lunch sometime."

There was an unexpectedly long pause before she laughed, and said, "Oh, you liberals. I suppose you think we'd have so much in common because we're black."

"Nice."

"Actually, Jenny . . ."

I waited, wondering at her hesitation.

"She and I do have something else in common."

"Oh?"

"Willie called me, after the meeting."

There was another long pause. Mine.

"You don't approve," Sabrina said.

"She has enough troubles."

"I don't have much choice of men in this town, Jenny."

"That's not her fault, is it?"

"Nice."

"She's pregnant, Sabrina."

"That's not my fault, is it?"

"Come on."

"No offense, Jenny," she said sharply and with a touch of self-pity, "but you're one of the lucky ones—rich, white, and loved. Maybe you're in no position to judge. Maybe you shouldn't throw stones at the rest of us who aren't so lucky."

"Well, that lets you off the hook."

But after the flash of anger came a feeling of sadness.

"Please, Sabrina, be careful. It's dangerous to start attributing your fortunes to luck and your misfortunes to fate. You're going to get hurt, and you're going to cause some pain, and bad luck will have nothing to do with it. This is a deliberate choice you're making."

"Yes, well, it's my choice."

"Sabrina . . ."

"Later."

She hung up.

The taste of the pork tenderloin—and my conversations that day—lingered in my mouth, making me feel uneasy, queasy. I downed two Alka-Seltzer tablets before I went to bed. They calmed my stomach, if not my mind or my heart.

=== 13 ===

IN SPITE OF MYSELF, I WAS AS EXCITED AS AN EIGHTEEN-year-old when the night of the party finally arrived. As I slipped into sheer hose and a ruby wool dress, and piled my hair on top of my head and clipped on ruby-and-diamond earrings that had belonged to my mother, I felt myself flushing warm with happiness and anticipation. Granted, it was my sister's party, and the bridegroom was depressed, and Sabrina would be flirting with Willie, and Gail might be hurt, and Henry Ingram would offend somebody, most likely Smithy, still, dammit . . . I was thirty-three years old, and I'd never been married before, and I was in love, and I was going to have a perfectly wonderful time.

"Damn right," I declared to my mirror. "You look terrific."

"Second that motion." Geof came up behind me and nuzzled the back of my neck, producing goose bumps that slid down my arms like tiny massaging fingers. Every gland in my body stood at attention. He whispered in my left ear, "I like your red shoes."

I smiled at his reflection and whispered back, "If I click them twice, I'll land in Kansas."

"No." He turned me around and planted a careful kiss that would not disturb my cherry lipstick. "Please don't go away from me."

I leaned toward him. The hell with the lipstick. I was suddenly filled with an electric feyness, a feeling that together we could do anything, surmount any obstacle, follow every rainbow, climb every mountain, ford every stream.

"Please wrinkle my dress," I murmured, just as his beeper sounded. I felt myself go stiff in his arms, which was odd, since the electricity went out of me at the same time. Geof looked at me with something like desperation in his eyes, and said, "Oh, *shit,* Jenny."

I put on my coat and walked him out to his police sedan.

We weren't saying much. The call was for a reported homicide. There wasn't much to say. I could hardly whine, "How can you go to a murder when you've got a party to attend?"

"Geof, I don't want to go to the party alone."

He opened the passenger door for me. "Then come to mine."

We got in, and he started the ignition. At the first intersection he hit the red light and siren. As we passed the street that would have taken us to Sherry's, I looked up at the three-quarter moon in the sky. It looked like a dime held between the thumb and forefinger of God. Flip. Heads you win, tails you lose. God had flipped that dime while we weren't looking, and it had come up tails.

Somebody had lost it all.

It was the stone house with the guttering coming off, where Mrs. Gleason, twenty-five years old, lived with her husband and five children. Still lived? Had lived? Died?

I stayed in the car while Geof raced inside.

Police cars, sirens buzzing, were converging like flies on dead meat. Neighbors were piling out of their houses to stand along the curbs. Any moment, the television cameras would arrive. It was quickly becoming a festival of sorts. Willie Henderson screeched up in his sedan and sprinted toward the house. I thought of Gail, all dressed up and no place to go.

I switched off the dispatcher's voice, turned on the car radio. There was a talk show playing, with a well-known author explaining how he got his ideas. I laid my head against the back of the seat and closed my eyes to the screaming reality around me.

I figured it was Mr. Gleason who was dead. Didn't know why I felt that so strongly, maybe it was because of the aura of "survivor" about the fat black woman in the yellow tent dress.

Where were the children now, those solemn children?

In my imagination, they peeked out from the windows of the little stone house. Huge, dark, frightened eyes rising like black moons in the windows. The eyes grew larger and larger, asking silently: Is it safe now? Is it safe now? Is it safe to come out now? In the back of my mind, a woman's voice began to croon in a deep voice of great sorrow and dignity:

> *Hush little children, don't you cry.*
> *Mama's killed daddy, 'bye, 'bye, 'bye.*

" 'Bye, 'bye, 'bye," the children sang.

On the radio, the famous writer said, "And sometimes my ideas just seem to spring out of thin air."

I opened my eyes, sat up.

You and me both, buddy, I thought.

They were bringing Mrs. Gleason out of the little stone house, but it was taking three of them to do it because she was wobbling drunk and singing the "Battle Hymn of the Republic" at the top of her voice.

"He is tramplin' out the vintage where the grapes of wrath are stored!"

So much for deep sorrow and dignity. She'd been into the vintage, all right, and it looked as if the grapes had unstored the wrath.

"He has loosed the fatef'l lightnin' of his ter'ble swift sword!"

"The man's *dead*," she screamed to her neighbors, causing the cops who supported her to lurch and buckle under her weight. Somehow they kept her upright as she flailed her arms and shouted, "That man ain't never gonna mess with me nor my kids no more!"

"You do it, Lanny?" someone, a man, yelled.

"Must of," she bellowed back. "Been wishin' that man dead for *years!*"

Then she collapsed onto the sidewalk, bringing the cops down with her. Her vast brown arms and legs splayed out over them like logs; her yellow tent dress covered them all like a tarpaulin; her eyes were closed, her head rolled back and forth on the pavement, and she was smiling. Some of the neighbors hooted and whistled. As I watched the cops struggle up from beneath her, I decided to go to the party alone, after all. Marriage was beginning to look like the prize in a pig-calling contest.

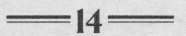

14

I HAD HARDLY REMOVED MY FINGER FROM MY SISTER'S doorbell when Sherry flung wide her front door.

"Get in here!" she hissed. "I can't believe you're so late! I don't know what to say to these strange people! They're your friends! You talk to them!"

She grasped my forearm to drag me into the entryway after her. But then she gasped and splayed her hands on her rib cage under her breasts. She had on an Egyptian sort of dress, white, with lots of pleats and gold trim, and a piece of twisty gold jewelry in her hair. With her face also twisted, but in evident pain, she looked like Cleopatra after the asp.

"Oh, God," she moaned, "that hurt, I shouldn't have done that."

"What's the matter, Sherry?"

"You're late!" she said through clenched teeth.

"Fashionably," I said, with an effort. "No, I mean what's the matter with you?"

She grimaced. "Cracked ribs, can you believe it?" I could, easily, having lived with little Miss Klutz for the first heavily bandaged fifteen years of her accident-prone life. It wasn't that she'd been a tomboy, far from it. My theory, often expressed when we were children, was that if she was going to walk around with her nose in the air, she was bound to trip a lot. "It's unbelievable. I slipped on a spot of grease in the garage and cracked my ribs. On Lars's tool chest."

I winced in instinctive sympathy.

But it was beginning to dawn on her that something vital was missing from the scene.

"Where is he?"

She started to screech it, but brought her voice down immediately to an intense whisper. "He'd better be parking the car. If you tell me he's not coming, I'll kill him! I'll kill both of you, I mean it."

I wasn't in the mood for hyperbole about death.

"He's not coming. I'm sorry. There was a homicide."

"Honestly," she said furiously. "Some people!"

That was a fact, I thought, as I followed her into the living room of her house, which had been designed by a disciple of Frank Lloyd Wright, a claim to fame that I had only just managed to keep her from engraving on a brass plate and sticking by the front door. The disciple's name must have been Peter, because the house betrayed the master three times before the visitor even reached the kitchen: The ceilings soared too high for human proportion; the building materials could only have been native to a foundry; and there wasn't any of that built-in furniture that makes a Wright house seem so deceptively plain and simple. As my wedding was supposed to be. Sherry had littered her landscape with gilded white French provincial reproductions that looked as if they ought to be covered in plastic. In her white-and-gold dress, she matched the furniture. I would have liked to think it was only an embarrassing coincidence.

She paused dramatically, almost causing me to run into her back, on the steps leading down into her living room. In the far corner there was a hired bartender. In the opposite corner there was an impressive buffet that looked heavy with lobster and other seafood. There was a man in a tuxedo playing a cello. There was a young woman in a brief maid's costume circulating about the room with champagne in tall goblets. My friends appeared slightly underdressed.

"The good crystal?" I murmured.

"They break it, you buy it."

"Jenny!" *"Where've you been?"* *"Where's Geof?"*

Cries of welcome and congratulations greeted me.

I looked down at the expectant, smiling, upturned faces. They didn't know about the murder yet. I was momentarily tempted not to tell them and to let them go ahead and enjoy the evening, but then I realized I would have to explain Geof's absence.

Sabrina Johnson was spectacular this night in a black turban, high heels, a gold chain-mail necklace, dangling gold earrings, and a short black dress as tight as a mummy's wrapping. As poor as the Gleasons were, Sabrina surely would have seen them in her office at the social welfare agency. Tommy Nichol, in a suede sport coat the color of raspberry sherbet, was standing close enough to touch hands with a plain-faced young man in a lemon suit. Had Tommy counseled Mr. Gleason? There was Kathy Ingram, looking surprisingly sexy in an emerald dress with a plunging décolletage. My big, blond brother-in-law was bending toward her. Another death, another statistic for the Ingrams. Henry, looking rather distinguished in a blue suit, was gazing up at me through a cloud of cigar smoke. Smithy Leigh was a surprise in a dress. The display of her legs, from hem to shoes, looked odd, as if they belonged to someone else and she'd only borrowed them for the evening. She'd be distraught when she heard about the Gleasons. Near her there was an attractive red-haired woman I'd never seen before, standing beside an equally attractive middle-aged man. Friends of my sister's, I guessed, who'd wonder at the pall I was about to cast over this evening. There were other, older friends as well. And I felt the absence of Gail and Willie Henderson, who would not arrive.

With an effort, I smiled down at my friends.

"Well, she's here," my sister announced sourly, then turned to glitter falsely at me. "You'd better have fun, Jenny. Do you realize this is the last party you'll ever attend as a single woman?"

Holding her side like Napoleon, she fled to the kitchen.

I nearly stumbled after her. Until she said it, I hadn't thought of the quickly passing days in that way: my last party, my last week at work as a single woman, soon my last meal, last joke, last emotion. Maybe I should have been commemorating these moments, counting them down like a diver before she springs into deep water. Seven days, six, five, four . . . I recalled a man who, once he became elderly, began to call each new purchase his last. "See these?" he'd demand of anybody who'd look. "They're the last pair of shoes I'll ever have to buy." And then, when he was dying he said, "Buy me the giant size of laundry detergent, it ought to about do me.''

I took from the maid my last glass of champagne as a single woman and descended the stairs to be the bearer of bad tidings.

I joined the group that included Henry Ingram, Smithy Leigh, Sabrina, Tommy and his friend, and the middle-aged couple I didn't know. Sabrina moved over to let me in, but she didn't look at me. My entrance into the party seemed to have interrupted Henry in mid-tirade, which he resumed at once, seeming oblivious now to my presence.

"There is no such thing as a reformed batterer.'' He pointed his cigar at the attractive red-haired woman. "These men have violent natures, as basic to them as the color of their skin.''

"They're not all black, Doctor,'' Sabrina snapped.

"I did not imply they were.''

"Henry?'' I said.

"We reform some of them,'' Tommy Nichol asserted, but he sounded nervous, as if he was intimidated by the doctor, or was afraid of looking foolish in front of his lemon-suited friend. There didn't seem to be any need for him to worry on that account—the friend was gazing at him adoringly, like a political wife.

"That must be true,'' the red-haired woman argued with some spunk. "Why—'' she had an accent that made her vowels twang like guitar strings—"I myself know a woman whose husband beat her up, but then he stopped, and now they get along just fine.'' The thought didn't seem to please her, however, because she blinked, frowned, and pressed her lips together.

"Anecdotal,'' Henry said dismissively.

"Tommy?'' I said.

"Tommy," Sabrina interrupted, "how do you manage to counsel heterosexual men about their relationships with women?"

She had said it straightforwardly, and although the red-haired woman looked shocked and embarrassed, neither Tommy nor his friend seemed to take offense.

"Because it's not about sex," Tommy answered. "It's about power."

"Sabrina?" I said.

"I don't know." She looked depressed and sounded discouraged. "Henry may be right about the futility of trying to change people."

During the conversation, my sister had butted her way in beside me, and now she interrupted Sabrina. "If this isn't the most dreary conversation! I don't even want to think about such things, much less talk about them at a party, for heaven's sake. Anyway, it certainly never happens to anybody I know."

In spite of everything, I felt a thrill of anticipation.

Henry Ingram removed the cigar from his mouth.

I held my breath, waiting for him to let her have it.

"Statistically . . ." Kathy Ingram moved in quickly from the fringe of the group. Henry popped the cigar back in. Kathy covered her cleavage with one hand, and said, "It's true that battering shows up less frequently in affluent, white homes, but statistics can be misleading, can't they, dear?"

"Kathy?" I tried again.

"How lovely you look, Jenny. I was just going to tell your sister that women who have the money usually seek private counseling and medical care, so their cases don't show up in public records." Quiet, demure Kathy could sound surprisingly authoritative when she wanted to; it was at moments like this that I was reminded that she wasn't just Henry's handmaiden, but a scientist in her own right. She was saying to Sherry, "It's the women who can't afford that luxury who end up on the welfare rolls and police records, and that's how most people get into the statistics." She smiled sympathetically at my sister. "When you cracked your ribs, for instance, Mrs. Guthrie, you probably went to your personal physician for care. But if you were poor, you might have gone to a public hospital where Medicaid would pay the bill. And then you'd be in somebody's statistics."

Sherry had been holding her side again, but now she dropped her arm carefully. "I hardly think you can compare my little accident with—"

"Oh," Kathy looked embarrassed, "I didn't mean to imply—"

I always seemed to have a hell of a time getting this crowd's attention, but I couldn't just stand there any longer while they argued.

"Listen to me," I demanded.

They turned surprised faces in my direction.

"I have to tell you why Geof isn't here. There's been another domestic homicide." My gaze slid to Smithy. "It was Mrs. Gleason—I'm sorry I don't remember her first name—but it looks as if she killed her husband tonight."

"Oh, no!" Tommy said and he grabbed his friend's hand.

Kathy Ingram looked as if she might cry, while her husband puffed furiously on his cigar. Sabrina's strong shoulders drooped, adding to her depressed, if beautiful, appearance. But Smithy surprised me by taking it more calmly than anyone else. She only said, "Lanny?" in a mild tone, and looked more resigned than anguished. The redheaded woman and her husband took the opportunity to slink off toward the bar, where they were joined by my brother-in-law.

"Well, I give up," my sister declared, and stalked back to the kitchen.

15

THE PARTY DIDN'T LAST LONG AFTER THAT.

"I'm afraid this sort of thing may be contagious," Kathy Ingram said to me in her soft, gentle voice as she was leaving with Henry. "Just as teenage suicides seem to be."

"Katherine is correct," Henry said, as he helped her on with her coat. He sounded even more pessimistic than usual. "One wife reads in the newspaper that another wife has killed a husband. That plants a seed in the second wife's subconscious, the seed grows into an idea that becomes an impulse that blooms into homicide." I smiled at him, a little bemused by his flight into metaphor, but he was frowning around his cigar. "In other words, murder becomes an option she had not seriously considered before. It is especially appealing when the first wife gets away with it."

"Eleanor Hanks," Kathy said sadly.

"Precisely."

Tommy Nichol leaned over to kiss me good-night, and blushed doing it. "Maybe SAFE can stop the contagion," he suggested, "before it spreads any further."

"Let's hope." I shook hands with his lemon-suited friend.

"Nobody's SAFE," Sabrina murmured. "Good night, Jenny."

Henry Ingram held the front door open for her. "You women ought to be grateful to these wives for ridding the earth of these pestilential men."

"Oh, Henry," his wife said softly.

The others filed out, offering their good-byes and best wishes to me.

My wedding shower, with its explosive guest list, had merely bombed, rather than setting off sparks of any consequence. Or so I thought, as I wandered back into the living room and headed straight for the bar.

"A Manhattan up," I said to the barman, and he obliged.

The red-haired woman was sitting on a stool, between her husband and Lars.

"It's a shame," she said to me.

I nodded, thinking she meant the murder, and sipped.

"Your engagement party, and all," she continued, in a sympathetic, oozing voice. My sister, having evidently ascertained that all my "strange" friends were gone, came out of the kitchen and joined us at the bar. She had a dark drink in her hand and the dark look of a martyred saint on her face. Her friend moved over to make room for Sherry, smiled sympathetically at her, then said more crisply to me, as if reminding me to look on the bright side of things, ''But I guess that's the price a woman pays for marrying a doctor.''

''Doctor?''

I glanced at my sister, who seemed suddenly to find an interesting ice cube in her drink, and whose cheeks were turning an attractive rosy color. Lars rolled his eyes, winked at me, and walked quietly away.

''Still, there's nothing worse than a party down the tubes,'' Sherry's friend commiserated. I placed her accent in Arkansas or maybe Texas.

''Oh, I don't know,'' I said. ''There's smallpox.''

Again, she seemed not to have heard me, a trait she also shared with her friend, my sister. ''Well, *I* know, don't I, dear?'' She turned to her husband. Then she turned back to say confidingly, ''I have some of the girls over every now and then for a little party, you know? A little cards, a little gossip? I've tried to get your sister to play, but you know tennis is the only game *she'll* play! I mean, she'd fit right in—one of them's a banker's wife, and there's a professor's wife.'' She glanced at Sherry, said archly, ''Remind me to tell you *that* story,'' and took a quick drink from her glass. Once refueled, she chattered on. ''And there's another gal who's divorced from a lawyer, and then sometimes, we have this gal whose husband owns three grocery stores. Well, last week, I had everything fixed up so nicely for them, and do you know, none of them bothered to show up! I mean, they all had excuses and everything, but still! Believe me, Jenny, I know just how your sister's feeling right now.'' Quickly, she added, ''And you, too, of course.''

The man patted her shoulder understandingly.

I was staring at her, and the silence was getting awkward. ''I'm sorry,'' I lied, for lack of an intelligent reply, ''but I don't think we were introduced.''

"Perry Miller," he said robustly, and stuck out his hand to me. I took it and he pumped as if I'd just joined the Elks. "And this is my wife, Elizabeth. Honey . . ." He drew himself up as people do when they're about to pretend they hate to leave. He spouted the practiced lines at which long-married couples excel: "I think we'd better be going, don't you, Lizbeth? Baby-sitters, you know." He smiled with awful sincerity at me. "So nice to meet you, Jenny, and we're real sorry about this friend of yours who, uh, died. But we wish you all the best in your new lives together, you and the good doctor."

Miller. Port Frederick was still in many ways a small town, where you were always running into people who knew people who knew the people you knew. Lizbeth Miller.

"He's not a doctor," I said flatly. "He's a cop."

The redhead sucked in her breath, then tried to cover that startled, dismayed reaction by smiling busily and pulling her husband away from us.

"So nice to meet you," she chirped, her voice rising an octave, as my sister's had done earlier. In a voice that now cracked with brittle sarcasm, she said, "Thanks so *much,* Sherry! Talk to *you* later! Bye-*bye* now!"

But there was no mistaking the fact that she had just blown her friend's alibi all to hell. And all because my sister was too proud to admit to her friends that her future brother-in-law was a cop.

"You had to tell them," Sherry said bitterly, misinterpreting her friend's malice.

I debated telling her the truth, but opted for saying, "It seemed only fair."

She shrugged, turned away, and abandoned me once again for the wary, consoling comfort of her kitchen. I glanced out the nearest window, at the three-quarter moon.

"Tails you lose, Eleanor," I murmured.

"I beg your pardon?" said the bartender.

"I'm sorry, too," I told him, and walked off with my drink to find a phone.

Late Sunday night, I woke up to the pleasant sensation of having my shoulders gently massaged. Without opening my eyes, I rolled over to snuggle up against Geof—who had not been home since before the party on Saturday—but as I did so, a strong odor, a mixture of alcohol, cigarettes, and sweat, woke me completely. He smelled like a drunk tank. Surprised, I rolled away from him and looked up to find myself staring into his tired brown eyes.

"You were right," he said. "Eleanor Hanks lied."

"No," I said with regret, "that makes *you* right."

"Well, you had that photo pegged—those clothes were a little too sexy for a bridge party with the girls. She didn't go to the card party, she hardly ever went to the card parties. They were usually only an excuse at which her friends connived so she could see her boyfriend. He's married. That's why she didn't use him as an alibi."

"Can she use him as an alibi?"

He looked puzzled and frustrated. "I think maybe she can."

"You know," I said, "I'd been wondering why they needed five women to play a game that only takes four people. Didn't her husband wonder about the sexy clothes?"

"He didn't see her, Jenny. She didn't go home as she said she did, although she did run those errands, so that's why that sounded so plausible. She admits she always took her 'dating' outfits to work with her and changed clothes at her lover's house. She didn't change before she went

144

home because Dick was always passed out long before she got there.''

''Or maybe she wanted to be caught?''

''And maybe this time, he did catch her.''

''But you said her alibi holds, didn't you?''

''So far,'' he admitted. ''Although her lover might be lying, too. He says she was with him from seven to nearly midnight, and they have witnesses, because another couple—also married, but not to each other—was with them the whole time.'' Geof emitted a sound that, if he hadn't been so tired, might have been a laugh. ''We had to be incredibly discreet about these interviews. You've never seen witnesses so loath to testify, but they swear they will if it means the difference between her freedom or conviction.''

We were silent for a few moments. I was thinking, ruefully, how little of my fantasy had matched reality—except for the central fact that Dick Hanks probably had been an abuser.

''Geof, there was another thing that Lizbeth Miller said at the party.'' I concentrated on trying to remember it. ''She said she had a friend whose husband used to beat her, but that he *stopped* and now they got along fine. I think she was talking about the Hankses. Then she looked unhappy, and I think she remembered they couldn't get along fine now, because he was dead.''

''Having a lover doesn't sound like 'fine' to me.''

''No.'' We subsided into silence again. ''So, you're more or less back to the beginning on the Hanks case, but at least you've got the Gleason murder wrapped up.''

His expression of puzzlement and frustration increased.

''We can't find the murder weapon, Jenny . . . the gun . . . and now she claims she was too drunk to know what she was doing. She admits she might have liked to kill him, but she's not sure she did! And the awful part is, I believe her, I mean, I believe she honestly doesn't know. I sure as hell wonder how she managed to think clearly enough to hide the gun so well, as drunk as she was. She says she passed out in the afternoon, and the next thing she knew, it was night, and he was lying dead in the living room.''

He lay down beside me, groaning, with his clothes still on, and closed his eyes. The drunken smell of Lanny Gleason—and what it meant—filled the air between us. This was the first time he had ever brought the physical residue of his work to bed with him; it was the clearest statement yet of how tired and discouraged he felt. The depth of his growing depression scared me. When I was sure he was asleep, I slid out of bed and went downstairs to fix myself some coffee and to watch the sun complete its rising.

══ 16 ══

ON MONDAY I WOKE UP IN A DELIRIUM OF REALIZATION that I was getting married in six days. I hadn't picked up my wedding dress, I hadn't checked on our reservations at the restaurant where my father wanted to take everybody for dinner after the ceremony, I hadn't picked up the airline tickets, I still hadn't bought any shoes to go with the dress, and what about flowers for Geof's lapel? My father and his wife would arrive on Thursday night, and Geof's parents and brothers the next morning. Because of the homicides, Geof was unavailable to run his share of the errands. And I had to go to my own job—which was not quite as urgent as murder—every day until Wedding Eve because I was taking all of my vacation after the ceremony. Frantically, still in bed, I ran my hands through my hair, which reminded me of something else I had to do.

"Lord, my hair!"

I grabbed for the phone book, then noticed the clock on the table; it was only six-fifteen, an unlikely time to get a hair stylist on the phone. Why hadn't I made this appointment weeks ago? Because I was too cool, that's why, too sophisticated and blasé to worry about little things like lanky hair. I was only getting married, after all, just an ordinary little event that happened to me every day. And flowers! It was also too early to call a florist. Or the restaurant. Or to go shopping for shoes.

Geof stepped out of the bathroom, already dressed.

"What's the matter?" he asked.

"I'm getting married this Saturday, and my hair's a mess!"

He tilted his head to one side. "I think you look fine."

"Men! Wouldn't you know I'd marry one?"

The bridegroom got himself safely out of the house and out of my way. I threw on my business clothes, skipped breakfast, and flew to the office so that I might, with a clear conscience, take an early and long lunch break.

"Morning, Jenny," Faye chirped upon her arrival.

"Don't talk to me!" I snapped, not even raising my head from the papers on which I was laboring. "I can't talk this week! I'm going to be a bride!"

"I don't think it's a vow of silence, Jenny."

"Work," I commanded. "Work, work."

At ten-thirty, I slid the wills I'd been reading back in their folders and picked up the telephone.

"*Oui,*" the man who answered the phone at the restaurant assured me, "your reservations for twenty people at

eight-thirty on thees coming Saturday evening are confirmed under ze name of Meester James D. Cain.''

"Thanks, Fred," I said once I recognized the voice of
the maître d'. He had graduated from Port Frederick High
School a year behind me.

"Oh, is that you, Jenny?" he said in his real accent. "I
thought it might have been your dad's wife or something.
Hey, pretty soon we'll be calling you Mrs. Bushfield, won't
we?"

"Over your dead soufflé. He's Bushfield, I'm Cain."

"Oh, good." Fred laughed. "I've always wanted to see
you get married and raise a little Cain."

"One step at a time, Fred. Au revoir."

"Hasta pasta," he replied, and hung up.

Next, I called Margaret, the seamstress who was making my dress, my beautiful dress, my gorgeous creamy
silk-and-satin dress of which I daydreamed, the fabulous
dress that would cause everyone to comment about how I
bore a striking resemblance to Princess Grace.

"Oh, Jenny," she answered, in slow and doleful tones.

"Oh, no," I pictured water spots on the silk. "What,
what, Margaret?"

"I've been sick, Jenny, all weekend, and I was going
to call you first thing this morning, but I was throwing up,
and couldn't even talk, and I still really feel awful."

It was going to be worse than water spots.

"And I don't think I can get it done, Jenny, oh, I'm so
sorry, I just feel so terrible about doing this to you. I kept
thinking I was getting better, but I just kept getting sicker.
Oh, it's your *wedding* dress, you'll never forgive me, I'll
never forgive me. Oh, I feel awful."

My beautiful, once-in-a-lifetime dress, undone.

"Could somebody else finish it, Margaret?"

"Not all the handwork, nobody in *this* town, oh, Jenny, I just feel so guilty, I—"

"Don't feel guilty, feel well."

"Oh, now you're going to cry," she said mournfully.

"I'm not going to cry," I protested, blinking back tears.

"Oh, Jenny, I'm just so sick about this."

"Go to bed, Margaret! Forget the silly dress! Goodbye!"

I grabbed a handful of Kleenex on my way out the door, then raced to my car and drove, sniffling all the way, to Lars Brand Labels women's clothing store.

LBL was a big barn of a discount clothing store where they ripped off the labels and knocked down the prices of designer clothing. They did not carry wedding dresses, but then I wasn't looking for trail and veil, I merely desired a uniquely beautiful, reasonably priced, one-of-a-kind original design in a street-length white dress that would make me look like Cybill Shepherd. And white dresses are, of course, so easy to find in New England in November.

I threw myself on my brother-in-law's mercy.

"Help me, Lars," I begged in his office, nearly genuflecting.

After hearing my description of the dress I wanted, he looked worried, an expression I wasn't happy to see on his face. I'd hoped he would light up like the used-car salesman who's got just the red Plymouth station wagon you want right here on his very lot this very day.

"That's a tough order, Jenny," he said, frowning.

"I'm not opposed to beige," I countered.

"We're long on cruise wear," he said, "short on fancy dresses."

"And I don't really mind suits," I said desperately. "It

150

doesn't matter that I've worn them five days a week for the last ten years. Do you have anything in a nice white wool suit, Lars?''

"I doubt it, but let me get a saleswoman to help you.'' At those words, he finally did brighten, and I thought he'd just remembered where some exquisite white dress was hanging. "And I know just the lady.''

After a brief wait, Marsha McEachen walked into his office.

"Ms. Cain!'' She brightened, too. At Lars Brand Labels, it seemed to me they were all happy for the wrong reasons. "Look, I got the job! Gosh, thank you so much for your help!''

"I'm grateful, too,'' her boss said kindly.

I asked her to return the favor by finding me a wedding dress.

There were three white dresses in the whole store, and they seemed curiously out of date to me. Usually, Lars could be relied on to provide the women of Port Frederick with styles that weren't more than a season or two old, but each of these looked like something Jackie Kennedy might have worn with a pillbox hat.

"I don't think so, Marsha,'' I said regretfully.

"Gee, I wish I could help you.'' She looked truly unhappy. "You've helped me so much. I really love this job, even if Ernie does say it's nothing as good as what he could earn. But we really need the money while he's still out of work.''

"Is he trying very hard?''

"Sure.'' She flushed, and I felt as rude as I'd been. It was difficult not to lecture this pale, soft pudding of a girl. "I mean, he reads the want ads like you told him to, and he says he calls companies during the mornings while I'm gone, but he can't go out on interviews while he's watching the kids for me, of course. And then by afternoon, he's pretty tired.''

She was the one who suddenly looked pretty tired. I had been continuing to look for good child care she could afford, but had failed so far. I determined to try harder.

"Well," I said, grasping for the thin silver thread that lined the clouds of her life, "at least you've got a good steady job here.''

"Yeah, it'll be great for a while.''

"A while . . . ?'' I thought my brother-in-law had hired her for a permanent part-time sales position. Something about the way she smiled and ducked her head caused me to jump to the worst possible conclusion. "You're not pregnant again . . . I mean, are you expecting a baby, Marsha?''

She nodded enthusiastically. "It's due in June!''

I felt a frisson of dismay snake down my spine: She already had two children under the age of five, a violent husband who was unemployed and jealous of her job, and now another baby on the way. It didn't take a meeting of our task force to tell me the young McEachens were bringing to a boil an indigestible stew that contained enough volatile ingredients to blow the lid off the pressure cooker that was their marriage.

"Does Ernie know?''

Doubt crept into her pale blue eyes, and she seemed suddenly to be having trouble holding up the edges of her smile. "Well, I just found out myself, and I thought maybe I'd tell him this week.''

I fished a business card out of my purse and gave it to her. There was no masking my message, but I tried to say it lightly. "Listen, if you ever need a friend in an emergency, you call me at work or at home, okay?'' I took back the card, scribbled my home phone number on it and handed it back to her. "If there's one good thing about workaholics, it's that you can usually find us when you want us."

The pale, pudgy hand that accepted my card was shaking a little, but she managed a sweet smile of gratitude. "But what about your wedding dress, Ms. Cain?"

"Please call me Jenny." I thought a moment. "Let me talk to Lars, Marsha, and we'll see if he can special-order something for me by Saturday."

But he surprised me by saying no.

"Shut the door, will you, Jenny?" he said then, and I did, leaving us alone in his office, which was stacked nearly to the ceiling with clothing and fabric samples. "The truth is that I can't order anything right now, Jenny, because my suppliers have all got me on hold until I pay a few back bills. I wouldn't want Sherry to know this, because it's all going to work out fine in a few months, but things are a little tough right now. As you can undoubtedly tell from what's out there on the racks, we're living off present inventory until business picks up."

"I don't get it, Lars."

He sighed. "Please don't think I'm blaming Sherry for this, because I'm not. But your sister's an expensive woman to keep around, Jenny, God love her. I've been paying myself a huge salary—much larger than this store can support—in order to keep her in houses built by the disciples of Frank Lloyd Wright and in designer clothes that still have their labels on them." He smiled ruefully. "But it's been my decision, and I'm to blame, I take full responsibility."

I was incensed, but not solely at him. "Our party! She must have spent a small fortune on food and drink and extra help for that party. How could you let her do that?"

"How could I say no?" He looked harried, unhappy,

helpless. "I didn't want to say no. You're her only sibling, you're getting married for the first time, I like you, I like Geof, we wanted to do something nice for you." Now he gazed at me reproachfully. "How could I tell her that we couldn't have a party for her only sister's wedding?"

"Oh, Lars." I couldn't very well tell him that we hadn't even wanted a party in the first place. "You're a businessman, you've heard of budgets? At least, she didn't have to spend so much! For heaven's sake, why don't you ask Sherry to take on some of the responsibility, Lars? Dad spoiled her, you spoil her, she doesn't know what it is to deny herself anything she wants! Don't you think it's about time to ask her to cooperate in living within the available means?"

"Well, I think I can pull it off without worrying her."

"What about the income from her trust fund, Lars?"

"Well, she spends it."

"*All* of it?"

He nodded but had the grace to blush.

"I see. What's hers is hers, and what's yours is hers." I stood up. "Well, that's great. That's just fine. Don't ask her to make any sacrifices, Lars. Don't ask her for any help. Just go ahead and die of a heart attack before you're fifty. She'll be the best-dressed widow in town, until the creditors grab the estate. You make me angry, Lars!"

"You won't tell her?"

"I don't have time." I walked to the door and opened it. "If I don't find a wedding dress soon, I may have to get married in an old white slip."

It was a measure of his problems that my brother-in-law couldn't cap that with a rotten joke. I left him staring disconsolately down at his desk, tapping the tip of a pencil on an empty order form. But then I thought of something and turned back to lean into his open doorway.

"How's she feeling, Lars?"

"You mean her ribs?" His smile held a touch of chagrin, as a parent's does when he's discussing a loved but clumsy child. "Okay, except that yesterday she was walking so stiff and careful coming down the stairs that she tripped and turned an ankle."

"I don't believe it." I rolled my eyes ceilingward.

"I know she'd appreciate it if you'd call her," he said.

It was another in the series of unlikely things he'd said to me that day. Nevertheless, I played to his fantasy of happy sisters. "All right, Lars."

It was the least I could do for him. Not only had he and his saleswoman put my own woes in their proper perspective—which was way down on the relative scale of human troubles—but he'd also given me an idea. I would have been grateful if he'd also given me a good deal on a dress, but what the hey, you can't have everything.

17

MY SANGUINE MOOD LASTED ALMOST THROUGH LUNCH.
Or for as long as it took me to pick up two lobster sand-
wiches at The Buoy, give one to Smithy Leigh as a peace
offering, and start to eat with her at the dining room table
in Sunrise House.

"Smithy," I said through a mouthful of mayonnaise
and lettuce, "I've been thinking how so many of your
clients are pressured by financial problems."

Her own mouth was full of pink meat, thus limiting
her verbal skills, a point I had considered in my purchase. She nodded sharply and mumbled, "Right."

"They probably need advice on budgeting."

Still chewing, she nodded.

"Do you furnish it?"

Unable to speak, she lifted her right hand and made

wobbling motions in the air with it, like a small boat on rough seas. I got the message: not much.

"Counting me," I said, "there are two M.B.A.'s and one C.P.A. in my office alone, not to mention the other business types I know around town. I was thinking, I'll bet I can wrangle some volunteer advisory time."

Still chewing, Smithy made a circle out of her right thumb and forefinger; she might have been rating my idea a zero, but I chose to interpret it as "Okay."

"We could start with the McEachens."

She took another bite, nodded.

"She got a job, you know."

Another nod, and her eyes looked happy.

"Do you know she's pregnant again?"

Smithy stopped chewing and stared at me out of eyes that had gone round with dismay. Her throat convulsed, as if she were swallowing tacks. "Oh, God, no." She said it in a dulled, defeated voice, but when she wiped a napkin across her mouth, it was a hard, angry motion, as if she were hitting herself. "No! And just when they might have gotten back on their feet again. That's bad news, Cain, the worst. If you could see the statistics on how often pregnant women get beaten up by their men—kicked in the stomach, pushed down stairs, hit in their breasts—you'd be sick."

I pushed my plate away, already feeling a little ill.

"It's hard to imagine," I said, trying hard not to imagine it.

"Psychologists claim it's the extra stress, as if there's an excuse for anything like that," Smithy said in a bitter voice. "And they say sometimes it's jealousy, you know, the woman's focused on herself and her baby, instead of on him. But I say it's meanness, pure born meanness.''

"So they need all the help they can get."

"Marsha?" Smithy poked viciously at the tabletop with her forefinger and grimaced. "You better believe it, Cain."

It was a shame to waste good lobster, but we didn't either of us seem to feel like finishing lunch. We carried our dirty plates into the kitchen. I left her standing by the sink, in her brown trousers and brown shirt, to do the washing up. I decided not to ask her where she shopped for better dresses.

On the way back to the office, I raced into and out of two other clothing stores, to no avail, then flew in and out of the travel agency to pick up our airline tickets to Puerto Rico. Like a hummingbird frantically flapping its wings to stay in place, I hovered by the agent's desk only long enough to ask, "If we have to cancel at the last minute, what's the penalty, Virginia?"

"Your firstborn child." She smiled, shrugged sympathetically. "It's pretty steep, Jenny: forty percent of the ticket price on this excursion rate. I think you'd better go, come hell or high water."

Or homicide? Her exaggeration, meant to be wryly funny, depressed me. If Geof tried to postpone our wedding because of his job, I just might decide I didn't want to live that way anymore. And so the penalty for cancellation might well be our marriage. And thus, any children. No little Bushfields, no little Cain to raise.

I slowed my flight to a trudge and returned to my car.

It was one-thirty, and I needed to get back to the Foundation.

As I turned the key in the ignition, I felt a surge of

energy go through me as well as through the car. I wanted to get back to the office. I was sick to death of worrying about death and of fretting about a wedding that might not come off.

"Home, James," I said to the car.

It was true: Work was home to me. I was glad to be returning that afternoon to a job that was always there when I needed it, unlike some cops I might name.

He was on the phone when I walked into the office.

"Geof on line two," my secretary announced, smiling.

"Thanks, Faye." I didn't hurry to pick up the phone, but took my time removing my overcoat, putting down my purse, getting settled in the chair behind my desk. I was thumbing through the other pink telephone message slips as I said hello.

"Don't ever say I don't do you any favors."

"What have you done for me lately?"

"I did what you asked and got Ernie McEachen an interview at the downtown store, and damned if he didn't bullshit his way into a job on the loading dock."

"Oh, Geof!" I put down the messages. "Thank you."

"They called him in for the interview this afternoon, hired him, and put him to work on the spot. I suppose the family business will survive one lazy punk."

"Probably. I picked up our tickets."

There was a pause before he said, "Right, great."

"What's my middle name?"

"Lynn," he said after a moment. "Blue eyes, blond hair, long legs. Loves cheese Danish, and cream cheese on blueberry bagels. Coffee black. Showers at night. Colgate toothpaste. Forgets to floss. Has mole on inside of left—"

I was laughing, which interrupted him.

"I haven't forgotten you, Jenny," he said then. "In fact, I'd say you're the one who's forgotten something very important, something so intrinsic that it goes to the heart of me."

"I'll bite. What?"

"That I love you," Geof said, and hung up.

Well. I placed the receiver gently in its cradle. So what if I had to get married in an old white slip? And we could afford a forty-percent penalty on canceled airline tickets if we had to—it wasn't like sacrificing a firstborn child, after all.

Feeling strengthened, I called my sister.

"How are you feeling, Sherry?"

"As well as anybody who's been eating leftover chips and dips for the past two days," she snapped. "We have enough crab rolls to feed several families, Jenny. If I freeze them, I won't have to cook for a year."

"I'm so sorry," I said for the hundredth time since Saturday; I'd tried it in several other languages, as well, but none of them mollified her, and I didn't much blame her. "It was a nice party, Sherry."

"How would you know? I'm in a hurry."

"All right. You probably don't feel like doing me any favors. . . ."

"Party favors, maybe, the exploding kind!"

"But I'm desperate, and it's just the sort of an emergency you can handle. My seamstress isn't going to get my wedding dress done by Saturday, Sherry, and nobody in town has anything appropriate for sale. And I don't have time to go to Boston. You don't happen to have any spare wedding gowns hanging around in your closets, do you?"

"You can't wear mine, I'm saving it for my daughter."

I thought of the yards of billowing tulle and netting that had enveloped her like a swarm of bees on her wedding day, and tried not to sound suspiciously sincere as I said, "Oh, I wouldn't think of it. No, I'd be happy with something short, white, and simple. Wool, silk, cotton— I don't care anymore."

"Well, you can come over and look," she said grudgingly. "But not tomorrow, because that's junior tennis, and not Wednesday, because that's my day for the hospital board, or Wednesday night, because that's always church guild and there's only Lars here, and not Thursday, because I'm arranging the flowers for the club dance on Friday. It will have to be tonight."

I thanked her and hung up before she could change her mind, or join another committee. I went back to work on Foundation business, involving plenty of my own committees, with my first job being to draw up a proposal to present to my trustees for a budget for the SAFE coalition on domestic violence.

At six, I left the office and drove to my sister's house.

The Guthries were just sitting down to dinner, which Sherry didn't invite me to join. She hobbled on her sprained ankle as far as the basement door with me, then directed me down the stairs. Even from the top I could see the huge old black trunks and long racks of clothing hung in clear plastic bags.

"Don't wrinkle anything," she ordered.

It was kind of fun at first. I felt like a little girl who's been let loose among her mother's finery. First, I plunged into the racks, flipping through dress after dress, suit after suit, pants after pants, coat after coat, but never finding quite the right combination of color, size, length, fabric, or style. For a while it was rather awe inspiring, this business of viewing my sister's plunder, but eventually it began to tire and depress me. Having failed with the racks, I turned to the old black trunks with a feeling of some dread. As I sorted through boxes of old costume jewelry, I realized I would never make a good pirate—I didn't get enough joy out of loot. But I kept opening boxes and trunks, hoping to find something.

I found it all right, although it wasn't what I'd come looking for.

The sight of it in the old black trunk rocked me, it socked me in the solar plexus harder than anything had for years. For the first few minutes after I found it, all I could do was stare at it, until finally I worked up the courage to touch it, to remove it from deep in the trunk where it had been buried, and then to hide it in an old clothes bag. I sneaked out the basement door to my car with it so that Sherry couldn't deny it to me. I didn't want anybody to see it until I'd figured out the proper thing to do with it—whether to bring it out into the open and take the chance of causing more pain, or to put it back quietly where I'd found it, and never mention it to anyone else.

I locked it in my trunk and drove away without saying good-bye, so that my niece and nephew wouldn't see me and ask their parents why their aunt was crying.

I ate dinner alone at the kitchen counter, fighting my sadness.

* * *

At nine-thirty, I got a call from a woman who was also crying.

"Ms. Cain?" I could barely make out her identity or the words through the sobs and whispering. "Oh, please help me. Ernie got fired, and I told him about the baby, and he's—"

She screamed, and the phone went dead.

=18=

I CALLED GEOF AT THE STATION.

"I just got a call from Marsha McEachen," I told him. "I think Ernie's beating her up again. Please, you've got to get over there as soon as you can."

"Give me the address again."

I did, and he hung up abruptly.

For a moment, I just sat on the edge of the bed and rubbed my hands together, feeling helpless. What if Ernie was hurting her this very minute? What if he killed her? What if she killed him? Where were the children, what set it off, would Geof get there in time, had I caused it by finding jobs for them, why hadn't I minded my own business, what would become of them now?

"Damn, damn, damn." I got up and paced the room, wishing I could drive over to the McEachens' myself but knowing I didn't belong there, that I'd only be in the way of the police. I pulled a bathrobe off a hanger in my closet, put it on, and wrapped it tightly around me. Then I sat down on the bed again. *"Damn* it. Oh, damn it."

Too nervous to sit still any longer, I got up and started downstairs for something to eat or drink. By the time I set foot in the kitchen, I'd already worked out the tragic scenario in my mind.

Ernie had probably smarted off his first day on the job and the manager of the hardware store had fired him on the spot. Before going home, Ernie had probably stopped for a few drinks, so that by the time he walked in the door, he was loaded for bear, and there was Marsha—a big, soft, pale target for his fury and shame.

"Ernie! How was it, honey?"

"Easy come, easy go," he might have said with a bright, false smile. And then he might have slammed the door so the old house shook. "Who needs the stupid job anyway? It was dumb, they needed some moron to do it, not anybody with brains like me. I was too good for 'em, and they knew it, the jerks."

"Oh, Ernie, you didn't get fired!"

"What, are you on their side? I didn't do nothin' to get fired, they fired me, the jerks. I was too good for them, hell, I'm too smart for that stupid job anyway, it was a shitty job anyway, I didn't even want it, so don't give me any crap, and anyway, who cares what they think, who cares what any of you think?"

"Oh, Ernie, I'm so sorry. But we'll be okay, honest. It wasn't your fault. You'll find something else, something better! And we don't have to worry, because I've still got my job."

"Sure." He was sarcastic now, and walking toward her. "You're so *sorry,* you with your big-time penny-ante sales job, think you're so smart, think you *mean* something, you don't mean nothin', you ain't nothin', you ain't never been nothin', you stupid, fat bitch.''

"Oh, Ernie, please.''

Eventually he would have pushed her, or slapped her.

And that's when she would have blurted out: "Don't hit me, Ernie! I'm pregnant!''

"You *stupid* bitch.''

The children would have been crying by this time, as their mother stumbled away from their father. But somehow, maybe when he went to the bathroom or to get a drink, he would have left her alone long enough for her to find the business card I had given her that morning at Lars's store, and to punch in my number with shaking fingers, and to whisper her desperate cry for help into the receiver. But then Ernie would have walked back in on her, grabbed the phone, hung it up, hauled back his arm to really give it to her this time. . . .

In twenty minutes, my phone rang again.

"Jenny, this is Smithy Leigh.''

She sound calm, businesslike.

"We need a favor,'' she continued crisply, snapping me out of my fantasy. "I guess you know, the McEachens are at it again. Your pal Bushfield just called. He says they can't bring her over here this time, because she says Ernie knows where we are. So we need a safe house, and she asked if she could stay with you. Bushfield doesn't have any objections, he says it's up to you. I should warn you, it's not just her, but the kids, too. What about it, Cain?''

"Of course. Tell Geof to bring them right over.''

"Thanks.''

"Smithy, is she hurt? Have they arrested Ernie?''

"They say she's not too bad—a little blood, some bruises, but nothing major. It sounds like she was smart for once, and got herself and the kids over to a neighbor's before he could do much damage. And don't ask me where the little bastard is—he split when she called the cops on him.''

"All right, Smithy."

I hung up the phone and hurried upstairs to get a room ready for our guests.

It was a couple of hours before they arrived, and it was a pathetic-looking little band that walked through our front doorway. Marsha, bandaged about her face, walked in first, and collapsed in my arms. "Oh, Ms. Cain," she said, and laid her head against my shoulder as if she'd never rise from there again. I put my arms around her—it was like squeezing a pillow to me—and struggled to remain standing upright. Behind her, Geof came in carrying a sleeping toddler dressed in pink pajamas. Willie Henderson walked in behind Geof, with a crying baby in his arms.

"We stopped at the hospital first," Geof explained.

"I've fixed the other bedroom," I said, and led the way upstairs.

There, we tucked the little ones into the double bed where their mother would also sleep. We waited while she gave the baby a pacifier to silence his cries. Then I presented her with a nightgown and robe, and showed her where I'd laid out a toothbrush and towels in the spare bathroom.

"Did you get out of the house with anything?" I asked her.

Marsha, clinging to me again, shook her head. "They gave me a bottle and some other stuff for the kids at the hospital. I don't even have any clothes for us, or my purse, or any money."

She was starting to cry again, and I heard the older child whimper an instinctive response in her sleep. Quickly, I said, "Don't worry about any of that, Marsha. We'll take care of everything tomorrow, so don't even think about it. Just try to get a good night's sleep. You're safe now, and your children are safe, and there are a lot of people who want to help you. Will you be okay by yourselves now?"

She sniffled and nodded. "Thank you so much, Ms. Cain. Jenny. I didn't know what we were going to do, 'cause they wouldn't let us back in the shelter."

"What did he do to make you tell?"

Her red-rimmed eyes looked blank.

"Where the shelter is," I prompted.

"Oh, I didn't, that wasn't what it was all about, I mean, he'd been after me to tell him, but that wasn't what it was all about this time, it was about him losing his job and me being pregnant."

As we talked, I gently loosened myself from her grip and guided her toward the bed where the nightgown lay. When I was convinced she'd be all right there alone with her children, I joined Geof and Willie in the hall and closed the bedroom door behind me. But it quickly opened again.

Marsha gazed out at us with wide, fearful blue eyes.

"Can I keep the door open?" she asked.

"Of course," I said, and changed my mind about turning off the light in the hallway. Sometimes even nineteen-year-olds need night-lights.

We left her then and returned downstairs.

"Coffee, Willie?" I suggested.

"No." He shook his head. "Thanks."

"Please give my regards to Gail," I said at the door. "Tell her I haven't forgotten her, it only seems that way. Is she getting settled in okay, Willie? Are the kids getting used to living here?"

"It ain't Boston, but it's all right," he said.

"I'm sorry I haven't been any help to her."

He was on the bottom step by then. "Don't worry about it."

"After the wedding, there'll be more time."

But he was already down the walk, out of hearing, leaving Geof and me standing in the hallway in front of the open door. I closed it. We slid our arms around each other and clung together for a few moments.

"Do you want to ask them to the wedding?"

"The Hendersons?" He propped his chin on my head. "Nice thought, but no. Willie and I may be partners, but I wouldn't call us friends. He's a hard man to get close to, and I don't suppose I'm Mr. Congeniality these days."

"Let's go to bed."

He clasped me tighter and said in a low voice, "I wish I could do something more than *sleep* in a bed with you these days."

"I'm too tired, anyway."

"Liar." He kissed me lightly and released me.

He went on upstairs, while I remained downstairs long enough to lock the front door and turn off the lights. By the time I crawled into bed, Geof was already asleep.

While we slept, young Ernie McEachen went looking for his family.

═══ **19** ═══

IN HINDSIGHT, IT'S CLEAR THAT ERNIE DIDN'T MEAN FOR things to get so far out of control; or, rather, he intended to *take* control, but it didn't work. Anyway, his own life seemed so far out of control at that point that a few more degrees of chaos didn't, at first, faze him.

First, he tried calling Sunrise House.

"I'm sorry," the night staff member said, "but this is the answering service. I don't know if there's anybody by that name at the number you called, but I'll take your name and phone number, and pass it on."

"Bullshit!" he yelled at her, which she dutifully took down in her notes. "Don't give me that answering service crap, I know you're at the house, and I know Marsha's there, so you put her on this phone right *now.*"

The staff member, as instructed in such cases, hung up on him.

He called back. "Let me talk to my wife, you got no right—"

Again, she hung up on him, made a note of his words in the phone log, and then tried to figure out if she should wake up Smithy Leigh at home to get some advice about how to handle this irate husband if he tried again. Before she could punch in Smithy's number, however, he called back.

"Please, please." Ernie was crying now, a fact the staff member also recorded in her notes. "Please, I won't yell at you anymore, I just got to talk to you. I know you can't tell me if she's there, I understand that, but would you tell her I love her, would you do that, please? Just tell her I love her, and I'm really sorry, and I'll get another job, and I'm really happy about the baby, and I just want her and the kids to come on home, and that I won't do anything."

"I'll take your message, sir, but as I said, I don't know if she's staying at the house, so I may not be able to—"

"Please, just give her the message."

"I've written it down, sir."

When the staff member hung up, she wrote in the phone log: "Husband called third time, calmer."

Five minutes later, when she was just getting back to sleep on the cot provided for the overnight staff person in the office, Ernie called back.

"Did you give her my message?"

"Sir, I told you this is only an answering service, and—"

"And I told you that's bullshit!" The sweet pleading had vanished. *"Listen,* you goddamned bunch of nosy, interfering dykes—you got no right to kidnap a man's wife

and kids, you got no right to interfere in a man's family!
You got no right, you got no *right!* You listen to me, you
stupid bitch, you get my wife on this phone, or . . ."

The staff member tried to hang up immediately, but in
her nervousness and haste, she dropped the phone, and so
had to endure his screams and insults until she finally got
the receiver back in the cradle. This time she didn't hesitate to call her director.

"I'll be right there," Smithy said.

"But, Smithy, what do I do if he keeps calling?"

"Tell him his wife isn't there, and that you don't know
where she is, and that you couldn't tell him if you did
know."

"I *don't* know."

"So much the better."

"But what if he comes here, Smithy?"

"Now how's he going to do that?" Smithy said, with
an edge of reassuring sarcasm to her tone. And then she
purposely told a lie. "Just because he knows our phone
number doesn't mean he knows our address. And besides,
what do you think we've got all those locks on our doors
for? Relax, it's no big deal, he'll cool off, and I'll be there
shortly."

Before leaving her apartment, Smithy called the Port
Frederick police station and asked for Detective Geoffrey
Bushfield. When she couldn't reach him, she left word at
the desk for the officers on duty to be aware that Ernie
McEachen was making abusive phone calls to Sunrise
House.

"Do you want us to send somebody out?" the sergeant
inquired.

"Not yet, but stay alert," Smithy snapped.

"We'll try," he replied, with a wry touch that carried

onto the recording of their conversation. "Call if you need us."

The sergeant relayed a copy of the message to Geof's office. Willie, who had returned to the station instead of going home, intercepted and read it. He walked out in his shiny green suit to the desk and instructed the sergeant, "If there's a problem at Sunrise House tonight, I want it."

"You got it, Liz," the sergeant promised.

"And tell the dispatcher that, too," Willie ordered. "I'll be cruising near Sunrise House, they can raise me on the radio."

"You could raise the dead in that suit, Liz."

"Just do it, Sergeant."

"Done, Detective."

And Willie left the station to get back in his car. He headed, ready for trouble, for the general vicinity of Sunrise House.

Trouble, as they say, didn't take long to find him.

The way we pieced things together later, it looks as if the next step on the escalator of violence that Ernie McEachen rode was the front step of Sunrise House. By that time, Smithy was inside.

Ernie rang the doorbell once, politely.

Smithy went to the door and called out, "Yes?"

"I'd like to see my wife, Marsha McEachen," he called back.

"She's not here, Ernie. Go home."

He pounded the door with his fist and raised his voice. *"You lying bitch!* I got no home now! I want my wife! I want my kids! You let 'em out of there, you got no right! Listen, I don't have to see her, just let me talk to her through the door, all right? I won't touch her, I promise, you don't have to let me in, just . . ."

His words followed Smithy back into the hallway as she said sharply to the night staff member, "Wake everybody up, and get them downstairs, right now, and into the kitchen. They can bring blankets and pillows for the children, but don't let them take the time to get their purses or stuff, just get them down here!"

"Okay, Smithy." The staff member stumbled on the first step of the stairs, then raced on up to the second floor. Outside the house, Ernie was ringing the doorbell over and over; the women and children upstairs were already rousing. One of the babies began to cry. Smithy ran into her office and called the police.

"Abuser on the premises," she said. "It's McEachen."

"Has he got a weapon?" the sergeant asked.

"I don't know. He's pounding on the door and yelling. I'm getting the residents gathered into the kitchen downstairs, and I'll lock us in. For Christ's sake, hurry up."

"Have you got a phone in the kitchen?"

"I'll plug this one in."

"Call me back when you've done that," he said, and hung up.

Then he called the dispatcher.

"Get hold of Detective Willie Henderson," he told her. "And tell him there's an abuser on the premises at Sunrise House. It's that Ernie McEachen kid. We don't know if he's got a weapon."

The dispatcher raised Willie.

"Do you want a backup?" she inquired.

"Not yet," he told her as he sped toward the shelter.

Willie didn't turn on his siren or light but drove quietly onto the block, turning off his headlights at the corner and parking several houses away. He saw, illuminated by the front porch light at the shelter, the figure of a slightly built man.

Willie got out of his car and shut the door, trying to move as silently as his nickname suggested. He walked around to open the trunk, reached in, and took out a rifle. He glanced around the raised trunk lid and saw that the man was still standing on the shelter's front porch. Willie then loaded the gun with ammunition, stuffed extra rounds in his pockets, and fitted onto the rifle a seven-power scope. Then, using trees, cars, and shrubbery to shield himself, he crept forward toward the front of Sunrise House.

Ernie suddenly stepped back off the porch.

Willie froze where he was, hunched down behind a car. Through the car's windshield, he watched Ernie look up at the second story of the shelter, then to each side, and then pivot on one heel to look behind, as if he were checking to see if anybody was watching. Then he walked over to where a tricycle lay on its side in the yard, picked it up, and began to carry it around to the east side of the house.

Willie began to move forward again. His intent at that moment—and in spite of the sharpshooter weaponry—was only to stop Ernie McEachen, arrest him, and to draw attention away from the shelter by taking Ernie into the station.

Willie sneaked closer to the house.

He began to raise himself slowly to a standing position, and to sight through the scope, preparing to identify himself as police, and to command Ernie to turn around and put his hands up.

"Police! McEachen."

Ernie raised the tricycle and hurled it at a window, which shattered as noisily as a bomb going off in the quiet neighborhood. Willie lost him in the scope as Ernie crawled over the broken glass and disappeared inside the shelter.

"McEachen!"

Willie lowered the rifle and ran the remaining distance.

At the sound of glass crashing, Smithy called the police from the kitchen, as did several of her neighbors from their houses. She was whispering her report to the sergeant when Ernie shouted that if somebody didn't unlock the door to the kitchen, he'd shoot his way in. The sergeant, on his end of the line, heard what sounded like chairs scraping, and startled cries, which he perceived to be the noise of frightened women hurrying their children away from the line of fire. Then the sergeant heard two gunshots, followed by a sound like a door crashing in, accompanied by women's screams, overridden by a man's unintelligible shout. And then the police sergeant's line went dead, as mine had earlier that night.

Shortly after that, the phone beside our bed rang.

=20=

GEOF GRABBED IT, AS WAS USUAL WITH NIGHT CALLS THAT came to the house—very few people ever called me at two in the morning to request funds for their favorite charity.

"Bushfield," he said, and then, after a moment, *"Hostages?"*

At that word, which was an extraordinary one to hear in our town, I sat up in bed, too, and paid close attention to Geof's next questions. "Anybody hurt? How long's he been in there? Who's he got in there with him? What about weapons? Has anybody talked to him, do you know what he wants yet?"

He listened, then said, "I'm coming," and hung up.

"What?" I asked. "What, what?"

"Ernie McEachen has broken into Sunrise House."

"Oh, Christ!"

Geof began pulling clothes out of drawers and off hangers. "Somebody's fired a couple of shots, we don't know who, and we don't know who's in there with him, or if anybody's hurt, and nobody's got communication with him yet. Willie took the call alone, which was pretty damned stupid if you ask me, and now they're calling in the cavalry." He strapped his shoulder holster in place, slipped the gun in. "Jesus, what a mess that kid's got himself into now."

"He wants his wife and kids."

Geof was slipping on a suit coat and heading for the bedroom door. "Sure. And by now, he probably also wants an armored car, a helicopter, a jet plane, four passports, diplomatic immunity, a suitcase full of cocaine, three million dollars, and one-way tickets to Kabul." He had a hand on the doorknob when he turned around to say, "Listen, I'm sorry to drag you further into this, but you're going to have to do something for me—keep Marsha sequestered here. Don't let her out of your sight, don't turn on the radio or TV where she can hear it, don't give her the car, and for God's sake, whatever you do, don't let her near that shelter. I'll send somebody over, but I'm going to have them park outside until morning so they don't wake anybody up. But they'll be there if you need them. All right, Jenny?"

I spoke quickly. "Doesn't she have a right to know what's going on?"

"Probably." He lowered his voice, to keep from waking the little family across the hall. "But he's not getting near them, and we can handle this situation better if we don't have a hysterical wife on our hands. Let her sleep, okay? She needs it, and God knows she'll find out the bad news soon enough."

"Who's your negotiator?"

"You're probably looking at him," he said, and departed.

But he stuck his head back into the room.

"I'm sorry. I love you."

"Be careful. I love you."

He was gone then, leaving me with a heart that had tightened to the size and hardness of a marble. I couldn't understand how such a small, constricted organ could beat so damned painfully against my ribs. I felt suddenly in a league with young Marsha McEachen, just another one of the women holding their breath on the sidelines while the men of this world made war on each other. Talk about your raging hormones.

I got out of bed and padded across the hall to check on the mother and children. They were sleeping peacefully, the little ones looking cherubic against the pillows. No wonder he wanted them back. But why couldn't he take better care of them when he had them? Now, would he ever have them again?

It would be morning before local TV or radio had any news.

I decided that I should go back to bed, especially since I might need all my wits to calm—or console?—Marsha in the morning. I returned to the bedroom and took a couple of Tylenol tablets to help me relax. I set the alarm. Once in bed, I blanked out my imagination so that it couldn't keep me awake by playing morbid scenarios in my mind, and then I fell asleep.

I dreamed that a baby was crying across the hall.

"Damn," I thought, "somebody feed that kid."

Then I woke up and realized it was a real child, really across the hall. I waited for Marsha to make whatever moves mothers make to quiet their babies, but the baby just kept on wailing. The crying got louder and more insistent, and then it was joined by the crying of a second child. Knowing I'd be about as much help as a Band-Aid on a broken arm, I stumbled across the hall to offer assistance.

Shawnie, the baby, was about to roll himself off the bed with the force of his crying. I raced to catch him. The toddler was sitting up in bed, looking frightened.

"Where my mommy?" she sobbed.

I grabbed the baby as he tumbled off.

"Marsha?" I called out.

"Where my mommy?"

It was a good question, and in a few moments, I had a second and then a third question: Where were my keys, and where was my car? A hastily written, nearly illegible note in my purse informed me: "Dear Ms. Cain, I'm sorry, Marsha." With a baby in my arms and a toddler by the hand, I ran out of the house to look for the police car that was supposed to be parked at the front curb. It wasn't there, either. I finally looked at my watch, only to see that it was only about twenty minutes since I'd gone back to sleep.

That meant that Marsha must have been awakened by the phone call, overheard us talking in the bedroom, waited for Geof to leave, pretended to be asleep, found my keys in my purse, and then sneaked out of the driveway with my car. Tugging at the toddler, I tried to hurry back into the house to call the dispatcher to warn her that Marsha was probably on her way to the shelter to try to see her husband.

"Me dirty," the toddler said, pulling at her diaper.

"Me desperate." I picked her up with my left arm and started to haul her back inside with her little brother. At that moment, I heard a car pull up and park at the curb behind me, and I wheeled, babes in arms, to find the police car right where I wanted it.

"Down! Want down! Dirty!"

The baby squirmed against my chest and began to cry again, too.

A short, husky cop hurried out of the car toward us.

"What's going on?" she called out to me.

"Catch him!" I yelled, as the infant squirted like ointment from a tube out of my grasp. She saved him from the second fall, and then held him out from her at arm's length while he squirmed and cried. I set the little girl back down, but held firmly to her hands.

"Jeez, I don't know anything about babies," the cop complained.

"Their mother took off with my car, and I think she's on her way to the shelter. You've got to let Geof know about it."

She thrust the baby back at me and loped back to her car, handcuffs flopping against her left hip. I watched her make radio contact. When it was done, she gave me a high sign and peered out the car window at me.

"Let's take the kids over there," she called out to me. "Leverage."

"Is that what Geof said?"

"No, but . . ."

"No," I said, and began to back with them toward the house.

"Come on!" There was excitement in her voice. "They won't get hurt!"

"Mommy! Dirty! Want!"

I shut the door, feeling no pity for the cop who wanted to be where the action was.

First things first, I thought, and headed upstairs to change the first diaper of my life. It scared the hell out of me—I was sure I'd either cut off the kid's breathing, or I wouldn't get it tight enough and, somehow—don't ask for details—she'd drown in it. I didn't have the slightest idea, either, how to mix the formula I found in the little bag the hospital had given Marsha, but I followed the directions on the can, prayed, and stuck the nipple in Shawnie's mouth. It seemed to me a bona fide miracle on a par with walking on water when he instantly, magically, stopped crying. But that left the toddler, who was now dry on one end but still flowing tears out of the other. I tried kisses and awkward hugs, all of which she fought by going stiff as a door, and then I tried calling the only person I could think of at the moment who could cope surprisingly well in tough situations.

Tommy Nichol promised to come at once.

When he arrived, he took the wailing toddler away from me, kissed the tears on the plump red cheeks, and rocked her against his pillowy chest until the little body gradually began to relax, to fold, soften, crumple, sleep.

"Abracadabra," I muttered.

But now, with the child and the accompanying sense of helplessness removed from me, I began to really see her. I realized I didn't even know her name, and I couldn't recall what Marsha had called this plain, plump little girl. Like her mother, she had thick blond hair and a face as round as a melon; also like her mother, when she cried, her entire face got red, and her nose ran copiously. It was not an attractive family; none of them was physically appealing. But the children had some of their mother's sweetness. Looking at her pillowed against Tommy's chest, my throat closed over the thought of what her parents were doing to her life, and to that of her little brother. I was tired and suddenly near tears.

"Jenny." Tommy spoke softly over the child's head,

calling me out of my contemplation of the child's bleak future. I looked up to find him gazing at me sympathetically. "You'd be surprised how tough children can be, honestly. Kids survive worse circumstances than these."

For some reason that annoyed rather than reassured me, and I found myself snapping ungratefully at him, "Well, let's just make it as tough for them as we can, shall we, Tommy? Let's set up the burning hoops and see how many goddamned obstacles we can make these kids jump over before they grow up!"

He blinked, looking confused and hurt.

"Oh, God, I'm sorry, Tommy." I patted him in apology. "You're so kind to do this for me. I'm worried about their mother, that's all, and about Geof."

"He'll be all right, Jenny."

His facile comfort again triggered an unreasonable flash of anger in me, but this time I clamped my teeth shut on it. Instead, I said, "Believe it or not, I need one more favor, Tommy—your car."

His eyes widened. "Are you going over there?"

"Yes. I can't stand it. I have such a bad feeling."

He gave me the keys. I patted his arm again, and turned to leave.

"Jenny . . ."

I glanced back over my shoulder.

Tommy looked like a man who had something he needed to get off his chest—and it wasn't the child. I turned around to hear what he had to say.

"Ernie came to my group counseling session tonight, Jenny," he said in the tone of a reluctant confessor. "He was drunk. And mad at everybody. It was wild! He'd been out drinking with his buddies, and they'd primed him to 'be a man'—you know, that tell-the-little-woman-who's-boss sort of macho stuff.'' An expression of pain and guilt crossed Tommy's soft features. "So . . . so I tossed him out. Because I don't let them stay if they're high on anything or acting up. Maybe I goofed, Jenny. Oh, God, maybe I should have let him stay! Maybe this wouldn't have happened!''

"Don't blame yourself, Tommy."

"These guys are power-hungry!" He said it pleadingly, as if my belief might ease his doubt and guilt. He didn't have to beg; I believed him, all right. "I have to keep the upper hand every minute with these guys, or I'll lose the war!''

"Well, you didn't start this particular battle, Tommy."

"I hope not," he said miserably.

"You didn't tell him the location of the shelter, did you?''

"Tell who, Ernie? Gosh, no, Jenny, I'd never do that. She must have told him.''

"She says she didn't."

He shrugged and, for Tommy, looked cynical. "Well . . .''

I left him standing there with the child in his arms, looking as if he would sway all night long if he had to, both tree and cradle. The cop outside challenged my right to leave. I ignored her and sped off in Tommy's old blue Firebird.

=21=

As I drove, I searched the streets for my own car.

What did Marsha think she was going to do? Talk the cops into letting her speak to Ernie? Try to persuade him to come out? Try to get into the shelter to see him? I knew what she might actually manage to do—foul up the negotiations, at the least, or get herself killed, at the worst. And why, after everything that had happened to her because of him, did she still want to save the moronic, mean little shit?

"Ain't love grand?" I inquired of the night.

I noted both the disappearance of tolerance and the sound of disgust in my own words. I thought of Geof, with the responsibility for so many lives on his hands now, and with the bitter knowledge that none of this would be necessary if people would only behave themselves.

"I'm beginning to understand, love."

But I was a long way from understanding love.

"Where are you, Marsha?"

I'd never before realized how many silver four-door Honda Accords there are in the world, or at least in Port Frederick. No wonder the United Auto Workers were ticked off. Accords seemed to inhabit every driveway, to be stopped just ahead of me at every stoplight, to turn at me suddenly from other streets, and the sight of every one of them kicked an electrical jolt through my insides.

"Where *are* you, girl?"

I cruised the perimeter of the shelter, knowing I couldn't get within a block of the police lines and thinking she would have had to park outside of them like everybody else. Unless she rammed the police barricades.

No. Please.

"Bingo."

I saw it: She'd run it halfway up a curbing so it tilted into the street as if to display its roof, which gleamed without color under the streetlight. It was about four blocks east of the shelter on a residential street. The driver's door hung open like the mouth of an accident victim, and the roof light was on. I parked behind it, walked over and closed the door. The light went out. I stood by the car for a moment, looking around me, wondering what route she'd taken next to get from here to there. I imagined her running awkwardly through dark backyards, climbing clumsily, painfully, over backyard fences, stopping on the other side to catch her breath in frightened, determined gasps. Or maybe she'd simply walked dumbly, straightforwardly, down the sidewalks. Or, maybe she wasn't even there yet, maybe she was hovering, frightened, working up her nerve, hugging the darkness under one of the trees between here and there. Maybe she'd lose her nerve. I hoped she'd lose her nerve.

I summoned mine and proceeded to trace the route I thought she might have taken. It lay straight ahead, up one driveway, into a backyard, over a fence, through another yard, down another driveway—more fences, dogs, lights coming on in dark houses. It was logical, but it was stupid. And it was all a lot of effort for nothing. At the end of my quest, I came up against a solid wall of police and spectators, three lines deep down the block from Sunrise House. The neighbors had converged like believers at a revival meeting. It was a carnival. Lighted like day. Noisy with nerves and commotion and outrage and titillation. I'd sneaked up on a three-ring circus, coming in under the tent flap when I could have just walked in the front door like everybody else.

I didn't see Marsha.

I didn't even, couldn't even, see the shelter, except in brief glimpses between the bodies of the spectators. It was first come, first see. They'd staked their claims to ringside seats. Nobody who had a good seat was moving out of it.

I walked the edges of the crowd, feeling frustrated.

A television crew was setting up its cameras in a space cleared by the cops. I walked over to their van. The rear doors were open, allowing a clear view of their monitors inside. I edged up, close enough to see on their monitors what they were viewing through their cameras. It was weird, like going to a rock concert and only being able to see the performers on the overhead movie screens. I was hearing everything live, but I was seeing it as if it were a weekly cop show on television, scripted, cast, directed, produced, shot. My mind veered from the word "shot."

Nervously, I watched the little screens for the actors I knew.

Nothing was happening.

Or maybe everything was happening, offstage.

Where was the negotiating team—in one of the neighboring houses? Working out of their cars with a field phone? Were was Geof? What the hell kind of job was it that asked this of a man? And that caused this fear like a fist in my heart?

"Be careful," I whispered. "I love you."

There was a sudden movement of the crowd, exclamations, a shouted "Stop, stop!" On one monitor, the camera's eye was swinging around past excited, anonymous faces in the crowd, finally settling on a pale, round figure of a person who was running, stumbling, running toward the front steps of the shelter. On the monitor, Marsha's hair looked as white as her bandages, and she appeared a lot heavier than she did in real life.

Real life . . .

This was real life, I reminded myself. I was watching a girl run up the stairs to the front door of a battered women's shelter where her husband was keeping mothers and children hostage at gunpoint. I was watching her pound on the door, hearing her scream, *"Ernie, Ernie,"* hearing the police shout, *"Come back, come back,"* but knowing they were helpless to do anything but also watch her.

We all watched the door open a crack.

We watched her slip inside.

And then we waited. The spectators who could see the front door stared at it. I stared at it on the monitor. We waited for half an hour. On the monitor, there was no commercial, there was no station break from reality.

The front door opened again.

Smithy was the first person out, poking her head out first, then following it with the rest of her body. A cheer went up from the crowd, but it was quickly muted as a police officer grabbed her, and pulled her to one side. The door opened again. This time it was a young white woman carrying a baby. She was grabbed, too, removed from danger. Then came a middle-aged white woman leading two small children by their hands, followed by another young white woman whom I guessed to be a volunteer staff member.

The last people out were a trio: a short, thin black woman who was coughing and two youngsters. The woman was trying very hard to hide her face.

Startled, I stared at the screen, trying to see her better, straining for a clearer look at that face, but the camera was keeping a discreet distance from these women who used to have secrets. I wasn't absolutely sure of her identity until a police officer rushed up to haul them out of the line of fire.

It was Willie Henderson.

He scooped one of the children into his left arm and put his other arm around their mother, who held the second child's hand. The woman placed her free hand across her abdomen as if to protect the baby inside. The short, thin black woman who looked so much like Gail Henderson was Gail Henderson, and the children were, I had to assume, Willie and Gail's children.

"Holy shit," I whispered, and one of the news crew glanced at me.

"You know her?" he inquired, his pen hovering above his notepad.

"No," I said slowly. "I don't know them at all."

He turned away to more interesting interviews.

I walked around the crowd until I located Smithy. But she was being questioned, and I could only stare. She happened to look up and catch my eye. At that precise moment, there was a gunshot from inside the shelter.

People in the crowd began screaming.

My line of vision froze on Smithy, as if to eliminate the possibility of anything—particularly anything dreadful—happening outside of it. She closed her eyes. She looked as if she were praying. When she opened her eyes again, I had managed to move up quite close to her.

"Maybe we got lucky, Cain," she said in a shaky voice.

"Lucky?" I asked.

"Maybe he didn't shoot her. Maybe she shot him."

"*Lucky,* Smithy?"

"You know what I say, Cain." She was pale, shocked looking, unsmiling, and most likely a mirror image of me. But she said it anyway: "I say the only good abuser is a dead abuser."

At a shout from the crowd, we both turned in time to see a weeping Marsha McEachen stumble out the front door of Sunrise House. She looked confused by the lights and commotion, and terrified.

"Hooray for our side," Smithy breathed.

It appeared to be over.

I walked back the long way to Tommy's car, and drove home to find out the details from the morning newscasts on the television. The anchorwoman told me that Ernie McEachen, nineteen years old, had been shot by his wife, and lay seriously wounded and comatose in a local hospital. It had not yet been determined whether any charges would be filed against Marsha McEachen, also nineteen years old. There was no mention of any police officer having been shot or wounded in the affair.

"Still here, m'dear," I said to myself, and then replied to myself: "Never doubted it."

After the news, the policewoman came into the house and took the children away. I took a shower and changed clothes, woke up Tommy, and he drove me over to pick up my car. I thanked him for everything, and then I went to the office.

Once there, I looked at my calendar. It said this was Tuesday. The calendar said I was getting married on Saturday. It didn't seem possible. It didn't even seem real. Maybe if I saw it on TV, I'd believe it.

It wasn't until late that Tuesday night that Geof or I got to bed, and we even managed it at the same time. We lay side by side, sprawled naked on our backs on top of the bedspread.

"I'm too tired to get under the covers," I admitted.

"That's okay." He groaned. "I'm too tired to roll over anyway."

"I'm too tired to breathe."

"Too tired to live."

"Are you too tired to talk?"

"I'll try." He groaned again. "At least until my mouth stops moving or my brain dies, whichever comes first. What do you want to know first?"

"Ernie and Marsha."

"When we went into the house, we found him in the kitchen. He was bleeding from a chest wound. She said he told her she was 'killing him anyway,' so she might as well go ahead and go the whole way. She claims he forced her hands around the gun, pointed it at himself and forced her finger on the trigger. But she doesn't think he really meant to do it, she thinks he was trying to scare her, to make her feel bad and to get her to do what he wanted, and that in their struggle, he accidently caused her to set the gun off. I don't know how the hell a judge is going to figure this one out."

"How is she?"

"She is hysterical."

"Who's got the kids?"

"Her mother."

"Tell me about Gail and Willie."

"Gail and Willie." He sighed. "Gail and Willie. Willie has been suspended. Considering what we found out about Willie today, I'd say that Willie's tail is nailed."

"What did you find out?"

"One—Gail Henderson not only has asthma, Jenny, she also has scar tissue that was the result of broken ribs she suffered about a year ago when Willie took out some of his frustrations on her."

I was too tired to be able to accept information like that without having a physical reaction to it; on hearing it, I felt as if I too had been struck in the chest. It was suddenly difficult to find enough air to breathe.

Finally, I said, "Why was Willie so frustrated?"

"Two—he'd been suspended while his department investigated allegations of excessive force against suspects. Brutality, in other words. They began his first week as a rookie, Jenny, that far back. And they weren't just citizen complaints, either. Some were filed by his fellow officers, so it must have been pretty damned bad."

"You didn't know this when he was hired?"

"No." He sighed again. "Cops can be like doctors, you know, for good or ill, we don't like to rat on our own. So somehow that piece of information never made it out of Boston when Willie applied for the job here. Maybe they wanted to be rid of him, maybe we were a good dumping ground for a bad cop, or maybe they just wanted to give him a chance at a fresh start. What nobody considered, though, was that when he tried to suppress his violence on the job, it would explode onto his family."

We lay in silence for a while.

"Do you know how long Willie's been in Port Frederick, Jenny?"

"A month?" I guessed. "Two months?"

"Six weeks. And suddenly we have this explosion of domestic homicides in a town where they happen, but never this frequently, or this close together."

"What are you saying, Geof?"

"I don't know, it's just odd, that's all."

"Do you think she's safe with him tonight?"

"Oh, Christ, yes. He wouldn't dare touch her. Gail has never been safer with Willie than she is right now."

I suddenly wanted very much to touch Geof, to get near to the warmth, security, and decency of him; I felt as if crawling into his skin with him wouldn't bring me as close as I wanted to be at that moment. But I tried. I pushed the bedspread back, pulled the covers over us, and moved over into the warmth of his side. He put his arms around me. I would have liked to have gotten even closer to him, but we fell asleep without being aware of our passage from consciousness into dreams. It was the bedside telephone, ringing repeatedly, that awoke us just after sunrise. When Geof answered it, we learned it was not Gail, after all, for whom we should have been afraid that night.

When he finished talking, Geof put the receiver back gently.

"Willie's dead," he told me.

22

At Geof's request, I went along.

Gail was new to town, he pointed out, she didn't have any friends, wouldn't know any lawyers, might need somebody to look out for the children when the police arrested her for Willie's murder. So I went, to play the role of best friend to a woman I hardly knew.

"I know you think I killed him!" she exclaimed to Geof the minute we walked into the small rented house. Her hair was wet, as if she'd just washed it, her face looked freshly scrubbed, and her jeans and blouse were clean and unwrinkled, as if she'd just put them on. "I know you hate me, but I didn't kill Willie!"

"Gail," he said, "I don't hate you."

She went into a coughing fit that seemed to grate on the nerves of the cops that were crowded into that tiny living room. I went to sit beside her on the couch. Still coughing, she looked at me as if she barely recognized me, which could have been true, since we had only met twice before. I wondered where the children were. I also wondered where Willie was. Willie's body. Tentatively, I patted her between her thin shoulder blades, but then I pulled my hand back. Finally, she stopped coughing, looked up at Geof again.

"What happened?" he said.

"We were asleep," she told him, her voice a high, rough croak. She spoke in staccato sentences as if she were trying to get the words out between breaths. "In our bed. Double bed. Willie was asleep. Beside me. I was asleep. Deep asleep. I'd taken a . . . Valium. Prescription . . . I have this prescription. Help me . . . sleep. They help me sleep. Woke up. Because there was this . . . noise. Explosion. I was confused. I thought maybe I'd . . . dreamed it. Or sonic boom. Something. Deafened me. I didn't know what happened. I sat up. There wasn't anybody there, but Willie was. He was. Willie . . . he was."

"Where's the gun, Gail?"

"Gun? I don't know. . . . Gun?"

Unexpectedly, she screamed as if she had just that moment discovered his body. We all jumped, even though it was only a weak, shuddering scream a doll might make if you pulled its cord too fast. Gail began to shiver. I put my arm around her tightly. The quivering turned to shaking. I felt as if it were only my embrace that held her bones together inside her skin and kept her from flying apart into fragments of flesh and bone. "Bad," she got out, gasping between the words. "Blood. Willie. Pillow. Over me. My hair. Nightgown. Horrible. Couldn't stand it. Washed it . . . out. Horrible. It was . . . so . . . horrible.''

She clawed at her chest, as if to rip it open to let air in.

''Where's your inhalator?'' I asked her in a loud voice, and she pointed wildly toward the left. Geof ran in that direction, and soon I heard the sound of plastic pill bottles falling to a tile floor. He came running back in with a plastic inhalator, which he thrust at her. She placed the mouthpiece between her lips and sucked in deeply, her eyes wide and staring. She did it a second time, and a third. But she was still frantically gasping for air when she removed the mouthpiece. It fell to her lap.

''Breathe,'' she gasped. ''Can't.''

Geof lifted her from the couch and started out the door with her, shouting instructions as he ran: ''Call the hospital. Tell them I'm bringing them a pregnant woman who's having a serious asthma attack. I need a driver!'' A uniformed officer ran out of the house behind Geof and Gail, and in a few seconds we heard doors slam and a siren start up.

I sat on the couch until it occurred to me I was in the way.

When I inquired about the children, one of the cops told me they had gone to a neighbor's until the grandparents could make it down from Boston.

''Poor kids,'' I said to myself.

''Yeah.'' The cop heard me and shook his head. ''God shouldn't trust them to us adults. Kids ought to be born ready to run, like calves, so they can get the hell away from us.''

They were bringing Willie's body out of a back room.

I left immediately and set off for Sabrina's house.

* * *

It was about a three-mile walk.

You can do a lot of thinking in three slow miles, one mile per dead husband. Three dead husbands in two weeks. And it might turn out to be four, if Ernie McEachen didn't pull through. The fact that he had lived through the attack wasn't the only thing that made him exceptional. For once, they had the gun that killed him. For once, they had a wife who admitted pulling the trigger. Sort of. Guns were not usually the weapon of choice for women, and yet here were four wives using four guns on four husbands. A contagion, as Kathy Ingram had suggested? If so, it was being spread by a virulent bacteria, some powerful, catalytic force that destroyed the women's immune system and contaminated them with their husband's violence. I had the feeling of a powerful, unseen, and murderous agent at work in the troubled marriages of our town.

Maybe the death of Willie Henderson would end the plague.

But if it didn't, who'd be next?

I reached the front steps of Sabrina's duplex and knocked.

"Jenny!" Her smile was unexpectedly warm, even welcoming. She was wearing a full-length white bathrobe and no makeup, and her hair was pulled back in a ponytail. She looked lovely. I felt haggard, just looking at her. Her eyes were shining with what appeared to be happiness, or some inner source of peace. "Oh, don't look so scared, Jenny, everything's okay now. Come on in!"

I followed her into the living room.

Like its owner, it was sleek, chic, displaying a bold taste in strong colors and modern accessories. She headed for the kitchen, saying she was going for coffee. I sat on the edge of her white leather couch. Sabrina didn't travel, didn't invest; she spent almost all of her relatively small salary on clothes and furnishings. It seemed to imply breathtaking trust in the future—or none at all.

She came back in a few minutes, handed me a white mug, and offered cream and sugar.

"No," I said.

"Don't be angry," she said, and smiled. She sat down next to me on the white couch and smiled again. "I didn't do it, Jenny, I told him no. You see, I got to thinking about what you'd said—about luck and fate—and about self-pity, too. And, I couldn't say this to just anyone, but I can tell you. I got to thinking about poor, deprived little Sabrina, and how all the poor little thing had was good looks, and intelligence, and an education, and loving parents, and great athletic ability, and a decent job, and wasn't it just a shame how terribly deprived she was?" She shook her head and laughed. "And then I thought about *him*—that little old, scrawny, ugly thing who wanted to cheat on his pregnant wife. And I thought, Jesus, Sabrina, what's the *matter* with you? So, don't look as if you've just lost a friend, Jenny, because believe me, you've got one for life."

I put the coffee cup on the glass table in front of the couch.

"Then you won't be so hurt by what I came to tell you," I said. "Willie's dead, Sabrina. It looks as if Gail shot and killed him last night while he slept. That's what I came to tell you."

She sucked in her breath at my announcement, and her hands jerked, so that coffee spilled over onto the pristine white robe, spreading a brown stain. Quickly, she got up from the couch, carrying her cup and saucer, saying something about getting the stain out. She was gone, in the kitchen, a long time. When she came back, the stain was gone, and the peaceful look had returned to her eyes.

"It's funny, but I feel kind of the way I did when my ex-husband died," she said, easing herself gracefully down on her white couch. "That was just a couple of years ago. He got in one fight too many, I guess. And I remember that most of what I felt was just . . . relief. You know, Jenny, maybe the world's just better off without some people. Some men. Maybe it's for the best."

I was exhausted, filled with chaotic, disturbing images of Gail Henderson and her two children I'd never met, and I was suddenly angry, as well, though I tried to tamp it down.

"That's not how you felt Saturday night, Sabrina."

"Well." She smiled, not the cynical half smile I was used to, but a warm, wide, sympathetic smile that relaxed her whole face. She looked extremely beautiful. "I've been wrong about other things, haven't I?"

And this is just one more, I thought furiously. But all I said was, "I don't know, Sabrina. I'm tired. I'm going home." I could have asked her for a ride, hell, I could have called a taxi. But I was upset, confused. I wanted to stomp home by myself, like some stubborn child who'd rather do it himself.

Talk about your self-pity.

It piled up further when I discovered the two messages that were waiting for me on the telephone answering machine at home.

"I'm calling from the hospital," Geof's voice said. "I thought you'd want to know that Gail will be okay, although they're not sure about the baby. There's some worry about whether it got enough oxygen while she had that attack. And she's under sedation now, which isn't wonderful for a fetus either, I guess.''

The message continued, as if he were conversing with me.

"What I can't understand is how she got rid of that gun so completely and so quickly, unless maybe she planned the whole thing. Well. My gun will soon be missing from our house, too. That's my wedding present to you, love. What happened with Willie is what stress can do to a cop, and I don't want it. No more late nights. No more busted parties. No more lonely weekends. I quit. Finis. Ten-four. Over and out.''

I thought that was all, but after the tape played in silence for a couple of seconds, there was Geof's voice again, sounding bewildered, angry, exhausted.

"What the hell's going on around here, Jenny? This is three domestic homicides in two weeks. Maybe it's in the water. Fluoride causes homicide.'' There was another silence while the tape played, and I waited. "Jesus,'' he said finally, "don't brush your teeth. I'll buy some bottled water. What the *hell* is going on around here?''

I waited, but the next voice I heard on the tape was my sister's.

"Where *are* you at this hour of the morning? In the shower? Get out of there and call me immediately! The more I think about this, the more furious I get! Call me as soon as you get this message, do you hear me?''

I started to call her, but then it occurred to me that she might have found out about what I had discovered in the old trunk in her basement, and that's why she was so upset. I didn't have the heart to face that argument this morning, so instead of returning Sherry's call, I made a pot of coffee.

When it was perked, I drank three cups of it in a row.

You can do a lot of thinking on three cups of coffee. Fast thinking, very fast thinking. It doesn't necessarily lead you to any welcome conclusions.

=== 23 ===

I DECIDED I'D BETTER HAVE IT OUT WITH SHERRY.

But when I called her, she didn't give me a chance to explain my side of things.

"Your *friend*," she exclaimed immediately, furiously, when I reached her, "your *friend* Kathy Ingram called me yesterday morning to ask if her husband, that awful man, could stop by. Well, of course I said yes, I mean I didn't know, I mean the man's a professional man, a doctor, of course I invited him over. Jenny! He sat down in my house, and I gave the man coffee . . . I gave him *coffee* in my own *house*, and he seemed so interested in me and Lars, just so interested in our lives—where had we gone to school, what sort of families did we come from, how was the business doing? Well I just talked on and on, innocent me! Until finally he started asking *questions*, like did we *argue* very much, did Lars *drink,* did I drink, how did I crack my ribs? Your *friends* seem to have gotten it into their heads that just because I have a few bruises, my husband beats me! That man, that Henry person had the *nerve,* the . . . the *nerve* to try to interview me for their study on violent marriages! I set him straight, you can certainly believe I set that man straight, but it was obvious he didn't *believe* me! Not only that, but your *friend,* that gay boy, called while I was out yesterday! Is he going to invite my husband to that group he has? I'll call *him* back on a cold day in hell! And not only that, but that dumpy woman with all the hair, what's her name?"

"Do you mean Smithy?"

"She called here, too, to invite me to her shelter, I suppose!"

"Sherry . . ."

"And as if that's not enough, my doctor, my own *physician* is asking funny questions about these accidents I've had! I feel absolutely humiliated, Jenny. I mean, outside of Mother's going to pieces and Dad's making the company go bankrupt and then marrying that floozy—not to mention you marrying a cop—this is just the most embarrassing thing that has ever happened to me, and I expect you to set your friends straight before they breathe a word of this to anybody. Do you hear me?"

"Yes, Sherry."

"Good!" Her phone slammed down.

I called Tommy Nichol at his office at the mental health center.

"Tommy, this is a little odd, but I'm returning your call to my sister. She's, uh, out of town, and she asked me to call and take a message from you. What, uh, what were you calling her about, Tommy?"

"I wanted to thank her for the party, Jenny."

"That's what I figured."

"And—" suddenly he sounded hesitant, embarrassed, a little unsure of himself—"and I was going to ask her if she'd give me the recipe for that cheese dip she served. It was fabulous. I'd like to serve it the next time I have guests over. Do you think she'd mind sharing it with me?"

"One twelve-ounce carton of sour cream to one large package of cream cheese and one package of Good Seasons garlic salad dressing. Make it the day before, and leave some clumps in it."

"Let me write this down . . . garlic . . . Thanks, Jenny."

"You can thank my mom for that. 'Bye, Tommy."

I gave Smithy the same spiel when I called the shelter.

"Yeah, Cain." She sounded crisp, efficient. "I'm always looking for funders for the shelter, and your sister looks pretty well-heeled, so I thought maybe I could interest her in becoming one of our sponsors. Especially since you're interested in us, I thought maybe that might convince her to come and look us over, maybe write us a check or two, what do you think?"

"I think you'd better leave me out of it, but I'll pass along your invitation, Smithy." It dawned on me that she would not yet have heard about Port Frederick's latest domestic homicide. "Smithy, there's been another homicide. Somebody killed Willie Henderson during the night."

She made a strange choking sound before she said, "What do you mean, 'somebody'? You mean Gail, don't you?"

"I guess so."

"I have such mixed feelings about these things, Cain." Her voice was shaky, and she sounded, for the first time I'd ever noticed, confiding and unsure of herself. "On the one hand, these men are no loss to society, but on the other, this is a terrible thing for the women and the children.''

Like Sabrina, she seemed to be reaching out to me unexpectedly this morning. Again, I couldn't reciprocate. Willie's words came back to me: ''You feelin' sorry for her? Maybe you want to remember, she ain't the one who's dead.'' I didn't repeat them to Smithy.

Two misunderstandings cleared up, one more to go.

I punched in the Ingrams' number.

This one, I felt, might require more than a phone call.

''Kathy?'' I said. ''This is Jenny Cain. Is there any chance I could come over to see you sometime tonight?''

''Of course, Jenny,'' she said warmly. ''I'll put the coffee on.''

Just what I needed, more coffee. Nevertheless, I made a date to see her at seven-thirty, thanked her, and hung up. Then I went to the office to face a day of normal, draining, hard work. It was a relief.

That night, in the Ingrams' rented apartment, Kathy eyed her homemade lemon pie as critically as a surveyor would a piece of land, and then she cut two huge and perfectly divided pieces. She dipped one of them onto a china plate for me, then one onto another plate for herself.

''I'm sorry Henry's out,'' Kathy said, and smiled. As usual, she was dressed in a neat, dark shirtdress that gave her an auntly look of prim efficiency. ''But that just means more pie for you and me.''

She handed me the plate, a heavy silver fork, and a straw-colored linen napkin. The napkin, which I spread in my lap, had been perfectly ironed by somebody—no scorch marks. Such things, the marks of deliberate, painstaking care, always seem remarkable to me. A perfectly

ironed napkin. Worth remarking. The pie, too, was perfectly prepared and delicious.

I said so.

She thanked me.

There's a chemistry to a friendship, every bit as much
as to a sexual relationship, and we didn't have it. As we
ate the pie and drank our coffee and traded politeness, I
tried to figure out why. I'd been working out a theory
lately that you could tell the state of a marriage—and the
people in it—by how their home was decorated. Too much
dark wood, too much red, brown, and black, or too much
generic beige furniture meant the marriage was out of bal-
ance, tilting toward the masculine at the expense of the
wife's taste and happiness. Either that, or the wife herself
had an undeveloped or unasserted feminine side. An ex-
cessively neat house, on the other hand, where knick-
knacks covered every square inch and all the curtains were
flounced, spoke to me of a marriage where the husband
only felt at home in the garage. The Ingrams' rented apartment offered no clues. The furniture was bland and beige,
but so is most rental furniture. It all seemed unnaturally
neat and ordered, but they were both scientists, and Henry
had always struck me as being at least as persnickety as
Kathy might be. There wasn't much personal decoration
here, they didn't seem to have brought much baggage with
them when they made their temporary move to Port Frederick.

"Where's your real home, Kathy?"

She paused in her chewing, smiled. "Wherever we
are."

It was exactly the sort of nonreply that made it so difficult to get to know her. I tried to pursue her further.
"Really, Kathy? Don't you have a home you go back to
between research sites?"

"Well . . ." She looked thoughtful, as if she were trying to remember something in the dim past. "We still have the little house in Cambridge, where Henry was living when I met him, and we keep most of our things there. But we try to make our home be wherever *we* happen to be."

I said the obvious thing: "How nice."

But while her eyes were lowered to her pie, I glanced around at all the beige blandness. They hadn't tried very hard. And it struck me that neither had Geof nor I tried very hard to turn his ugly contemporary house into our mutual home. Why? Because we didn't like the house, because we expected to move, because it had belonged to him and another woman, because we weren't happy there, because we hadn't yet settled in to being *us?* Whichever, the lack of color and warmth and small, loving touches seemed to suggest an emotional freeze, or a withholding on somebody's part, possibly mine. I wasn't sure I cared for my own comparison between this apartment and the place I lived, so I changed the subject in my mind, and got to the point of my visit.

"Kathy," I began, "I'm afraid there's been a misunderstanding."

She blushed, looked distressed, and put down the plate. "Oh, dear, this is about your sister, isn't it?"

"Yes, really, she's been clumsy since she was a child—this is nothing new. I'll grant you she doesn't usually wound herself so badly and in such rapid consecutive order, but otherwise it's entirely in character, really."

"Jenny." Kathy smoothed the napkin in her own lap. She seemed to be searching for the right words. "I don't know how to say this, and I wish I didn't have to, because I feel it's a violation of your sister's privacy. But . . ." Again, she paused, glanced at me, looked down at the napkin. It was obvious that speaking so openly and intimately to me was difficult for her, and she was, accordingly, awkward. I wondered how she managed to interview couples about the most personal details of their lives, but then I remembered she had the formality of the questionnaire to protect her. "We've had so much experience at seeing the results of family violence, Henry and I have, and through the years we've come to recognize the accidents that aren't really accidents, the coincidences that are too coincidental to believe, the denial that masks serious trouble."

It sounded like an excerpt from a speech. I smiled, nearly laughed. "Come on, Kathy . . ."

"Please, listen to me." She finally looked me in the eyes. "I know what your sister said to Henry yesterday, he told me how strongly she denied everything, how vehement she was, and how offended. And, Jenny, I'm sorry, truly sorry, that we jumped into this situation without preparing the way any better. You see, most of our referrals come from social welfare offices, so we were eager—probably too eager—to talk to a couple in the upper-income bracket. That was a mistake, our mistake. And I should have gone along to smooth the way, I know Henry can be less than diplomatic at times. But, Jenny, our intentions were good. We do take these problems personally, they're more than statistics to us because we both came from violent families. I know that's one of the things that drew me to him, that sense he exuded of *understanding* how bad it was." She was blushing deeply again. I felt moved at the courage it took for her to tell me all this. "I felt that Henry was determined to change things, as I am. We know what it's like for these couples and their children, and we're, oh, we're so sympathetic. I know Henry doesn't always seem like a sympathetic person, but he is, he is about . . . this. So, when we saw that your sister was hurting, we felt we had to do something to intervene. At the very least, we wanted to offer our concern to her. And our first impressions, Jenny, they were no mistake, Henry's convinced of that. There is trouble in that household, he feels strongly, and your sister is suffering from it.''

"Kathy." I was beginning to feel as frustrated as a suspect who's been accused of a crime she didn't commit. "All right, yes, there's some financial trouble, but that's it, there isn't anything else. She fell in the garage, she twisted an ankle—''

"Twisted an ankle? When?''

"Oh, Kathy, it was an *accident*, because she was walking awkwardly, because of her ribs.''

"How can you be so sure, Jenny?''

"Because I *know* her, because she went through her childhood in splints and slings and bandages!''

"Did your parents have a troubled relationship, Jenny?''

"Oh, God." I leaned my head against the sofa and closed my eyes. I wanted to laugh, but Kathy obviously wouldn't share the joke. To add to my problem, all the coffee I'd had that day was beginning to get to me. "May I use your bathroom, Kathy?''

She seemed as relieved as I at the abrupt change of subject, and she stood up to lead me to the hallway and to point. "Use mine, Jenny—it's just inside that bedroom, to your left.''

I walked down the hall past a gun display case and a linen closet, and on into the room at the end, where I flipped on the overhead light. It revealed a large bedroom that contained twin beds, two large dressers, a chaise lounge, and a vanity table. It was all perfectly neat, perfectly color-coordinated in beige, almost pretty in an unimaginative way. Everything was perfect and perfectly controlled, just like its mistress.

In the immaculate bathroom, I stared at my tired face in the mirror and considered how to break down that perfectly solid conviction of hers—the one that had her thinking that Lars was a wife beater—and get her to believe me. I supposed that it didn't actually matter if she believed me, I was sure they would keep their opinions to themselves and that they'd respect Sherry's demand for them to leave her alone. But still, I liked my brother-in-law, and I didn't want anybody to think such things about him. Or was it that I didn't want my sister to look like a victim, because that might reflect badly on our family? On me. I used the facilities, washed my hands, straightened my hair with my fingers, and wondered what it must be like to be Kathy Ingram, so sure of her statistics, so convinced of her opinions, so perfectly in control.

When I was ready to give it another try, I turned out the lights and started down the hall again. The door to the linen closet was ajar, and I shut it. The guns in the display case were gleaming, and I stopped to admire them. There wasn't much to admire, not as gun collections go. No real antiques that I could tell. No expensive rifles with beautiful stocks and barrels. Just mostly ordinary pistols and revolvers—a couple of little .22's, a few .38's and .45's like the ones that millions of good ol' boys stashed in their bedside drawers. They weren't even very clean, at least not compared to collections I'd seen in various cops' homes, and not compared to the rest of the house.

"Ugly things, aren't they?" Kathy spoke at my shoulder. She was smiling again, now that we were talking about other things, and she seemed to read my own thoughts. Maybe, I thought, we could develop a bit of empathy here, after all. "I'd love to dust them, at least, but Henry won't let me, he says it's important for them to remain in their original condition, that it increases their value to him. I suppose it's just as well, since I don't know a thing about guns, and I'd probably shoot myself if I tried to polish them. That's his newest one, right there.''

I looked where she pointed, to a shelf toward the bottom of the case. She opened the case, took out the gun, and turned it over casually in her hands.

''Let me see that, Kathy.'' Carefully, I took it from her. It looked a lot like the one Geof wore. Willie had been killed with one just like it, his own .38. My heart skipped. ''Jesus, Kathy! Did you know this thing's loaded?''

''Oh, for heaven's sake,'' she said, and shook her head as if I'd just told her that her little boy had knocked out my window with his baseball. ''That man!''

Moving even more carefully than before, I replaced the gun in the cabinet.

''For an intelligent man,'' Kathy was saying, ''Henry can be so absentminded sometimes! That's what he's doing tonight, too, getting another gun to add to the collection. I don't mind, really, they don't seem to be very expensive.''

''What kind of gun?''

''It doesn't seem to hurt our budget.''

''What kind of gun, Kathy?''

She looked startled out of her poise. ''Kind? I don't know, Jenny, I think he said it was a Colt something or other, evidently something new that he'd seen recently, and that he wanted.''

''Where, where was he going to get it?''

''A gun shop, I guess, isn't that where they buy them?''

''Has he added any other new guns in the last couple of weeks?''

''Why, yes, that one . . . and that one.''

She had pointed to a .38 and yet another .45.

Dick Hanks had been shot with his own .38 caliber gun. Lanny Gleason's husband had been killed with his own .45. All the couples had been exhaustively interviewed by the Ingrams, so that Henry and Kathy knew if the wives got regular nights out—and when—and which wives were so tense, like Gail, that they needed tranquilizers to sleep, and which couples drank themselves into stupors on Saturday afternoons. They knew who owned guns and where they kept those guns and the bullets.

My brother-in-law owned an old Colt .45.

This was Wednesday, Sherry's night at her church guild, and she had told me that Lars would be home alone.

I pushed Kathy aside and ran into the kitchen to the phone. First I tried calling Lars, but his phone was busy. Or off the hook? I called the police station then to transmit an urgent message to Detective Geof Bushfield.

Kathy Ingram was listening, and ashen.

She suddenly ran out of the room. But in a couple of seconds she was back, and she ran up to me and grabbed the phone out of my hand. I put up my arms to ward off the blow I expected, but she merely let the phone drop. Then she grabbed my hand and pulled me out of the kitchen after her.

"We have to save him," Kathy said.

I followed her, wondering which man she meant.

24

KATHY DROVE US TO THE GUTHRIES' IN HER STATION wagon, thus compounding my sinking feeling that I was rapidly losing whatever control I might have had. She drove wildly, madly, a racer on her last desperate laps, and I saw the tight interior control she usually had over herself leaving her, pouring out like gas out of a tank. During the run to the car, her dark hair had come loose from its pins, at some point a button had popped open at her cuff, her hose sagged at her ankles, sweat ringed the armpits of her dark shirtdress. It was as if an invisible hand had shaken her, rattling her, opening and loosening her clothes, her pores, her glands, her mind, her mouth.

"He hated his father. Henry hated his father, that's why he left home at sixteen, to go to school, to get away from his father, so he wouldn't have to see what his father was doing to his mother, beating her up all the time, holding guns to her head, but he despised her, too. Henry despised his mother for taking it, for taking it so that he had to witness it and be helpless to stop it, and feel guilty.

"I felt so sorry for him. I admired him so when I met him. But I felt so sorry for him, he was so lonely, and he needed me. And I needed him, oh, Jenny, I've always felt so protected around Henry! I needed protection, I never had it as a child. He was doing good work, it was important work, and I could help him. I thought I could help him. Why didn't I help him! I lived with him, and I knew him, and I didn't know what he was doing, why didn't I know! Those poor men, those poor women . . . ."

"How long, Kathy?"

"Boston—he brought home guns in Boston. Oh, dear God. And before that, before Boston, in Ann Arbor; in Bangor, before that. You saw how many guns, oh, God! All those guns, all those people, I want to die, I want him to die. Oh, I don't mean that—I don't want those people to be dead, I don't want your brother-in-law to be dead, I want to be dead so I can't know this, please make me dead, God, and kill him, please take him now, please take him ten years ago, bring back all those people and kill us, make me go to another university, make me go to another class, somebody else's class, make me different so I wouldn't want him, make him different so he wouldn't need me, make me die when I was born, make his mother drown him, make his father die before he was born, make him different, make me different, take it away, take this away from me."

She laid the flat of her right palm on the car's horn as if it were a siren, so that it blared us onto the block where Sherry and Lars lived. She drove the car over the curb, over the lawn, close to the front steps. When she flung herself out of the car, she was screaming his name as she ran, but the sound came out only as the strangled whisper of someone who is so desperately afraid that her larynx has closed, her tongue is paralyzed, and the scream pierces her own brain instead of the air where she aims it.

"Henry, Henry, don't. Stop, Henry."

I pushed past her, and she fell as if her muscles had given out on her, too, along with her voice, as if the invisible hand had shaken all the stuffing out of her, leaving only a quivering, twitching, epileptic shell of a body, like a locust's, on the ground. If I'd had time for it, I would have been horrified by the sight of the complete disintegration of her self. I shoved open the front door and, hearing nothing, forced myself to stand quietly in the foyer.

"Come in."

It was Henry's deep voice, calling from the living room.

In the mirror in the foyer, I saw the reflected image of Henry standing, holding a .45 Colt to Lars's big blond head. Lars stared back at me in the mirror. He was pale and looked puzzled, as if somebody had told a joke he didn't get, but he gazed steadily, calmly, into my own mirrored eyes without any trace that I could see of fear or panic. I thought he was the most dignified helpless person I'd ever seen, and I suddenly loved him overwhelmingly, this good man, this patient husband to my sister, this kind father to my niece and nephew, this good friend to me.

I was afraid to move, but I let my gaze travel to Henry in the mirror.

He, too, was looking back at me.

"You've got it wrong this time, Henry," I said to the mirror.

"You would defend him," Henry replied scornfully.

"He's a gentle man, Henry, he never hurt her."

"They all hurt her."

"Who, Henry?"

"All the men have guns and fists, and they beat her and hurt her until I stop them from doing it anymore."

"But you make her suffer by doing it, Henry."

"I don't care what happens to her."

"You love her."

"I loved him, too. God hates me for loving him."

"Because he hurt her?"

"She let him hurt her."

"It wasn't your fault, Henry."

"I know." He looked down at Lars. "It was his fault."

"Henry!"

It wasn't my scream, it was Kathy's.

Henry's head jerked up, and he was staring at her in the mirror as she pulled the gun—Willie's gun—out of her pocket and aimed it at him and pulled the trigger. When his face shattered, I expected the mirror to shatter, too. It didn't, of course. In it, I could see clearly the body on the floor and the blood that had sprayed onto my brother-in-law's face. Lars stared back at me, and I realized that it had not been dignity but the paralysis of terror that had kept him pinned so quietly to the chair. I knew how he felt—my own feet seemed planted permanently to the floor of the foyer. Kathy Ingram was the only one who was moving, and that was only to crumple again to the ground and to begin to weep.

"I saved him," she said.

I still didn't know which man she meant.

Epilogue

"JENNY, IF YOU DON'T HURRY, YOU'LL BE LATE TO YOUR own wedding," my father complained. With his Palm Springs tan and long silver hair, he looked even more than usual like some retired movie star whose name ought to show up in Trivial Pursuit games, starring in some forgotten movie opposite Merle Oberon. But he was only Jimmy Cain, the former clam-canning company president, forced out of business and out of town by his own ineptness. Still, he looked extraordinarily handsome, even distinguished in the tuxedo he'd insisted on wearing to this mostly unformal wedding.

"You look the role, Dad."

He flicked invisible lint from his lapel, smiling sadly.

"You young people have no sense of occasion," my father said, referring perhaps to the fruitless arguments I'd waged against the tux. "Top hat and tails went out with the British Empire, you know, and that has always seemed a great tragedy to me."

I checked myself out in the mirror on the wall of the church lounge. Yes. In my mother's wedding dress, the lovely cream silk-and-lace gown I'd found in the trunk in Sherry's basement, I looked the role, too. I'd finally told Sherry, and she'd cried a little, but she hadn't objected.

"What has, Dad, the end of imperialism?"

He sighed, seeing only his own elegant image in the mirror where we were both reflected. Maybe my mother couldn't be at my wedding, maybe in her semiconscious state she'd never even be aware I was married, but I'd feel her presence and her love all the same, in the warm soft embrace of her dress. My father hadn't seemed to recognize it, and I hadn't seen the point of wounding him by speaking the memory.

"I've often said it was the death of style," he said.

I touched a finger to the short, lacy veil my mother had worn when she had married him some thirty-five years earlier. It had covered her eyes to important truths about him and about herself, that veil had, and I could only hope it wouldn't blind her elder daughter, as well.

"Ah. Life is hard, Dad."

He suddenly brightened and looked at me briefly.

"Do you like the golf clubs we got you for a wedding present?"

"They're gorgeous, but we don't play golf."

He lifted his chin from his immaculate collar and gazed out the stained-glass window. I waited for his profound comment on this important moment of my life. He cleared his throat.

"That's what your stepmother said, but I said, 'Don't be silly, my dear, everybody plays golf.' "

"Let's go, Dad."

"Do you, Geoffrey Allen, take Jennifer Lynn to be your lawful wedded wife?"

Henry Ingram had knocked boldly at the door of Dick and Eleanor Hanks's home that Friday night. Dick, recognizing him, admitted him. Henry knew from interviewing the couple that this was Eleanor's night out, that they kept a weapon on the premises, that the gun lay in the drawer beside the bed. He had only to excuse himself to go to the bathroom in order to obtain it. And then he had only to call Dick into the bedroom, to shoot him through the muffling pillow, and to walk out the front door, invisible to the neighbors behind their night-closed doors.

"I do."

"Do you, Jennifer, take Geoffrey to be your lawful wedded husband?"

It had been as easy to kill Lanny Gleason's husband as it had been for him to kill the other men in the other cities, the other towns. Henry knew, from the interviews with the Gleasons, that they both got drunk to unconsciousness every Saturday night. So they never even knew he was in the house. Ironically, it was SAFE that galvanized him into killing more, and more quickly—SAFE fed Henry's sense of personal mission, that mission being to "save" the women by killing the men, even if it brought suspicion onto the women themselves.

"To have and to hold from this day forward, in sickness . . ."

Henry had not been so direct in attempting to kill young Ernie McEachen; he'd merely stirred the pot by calling Ernie, by telling him the address of the shelter, and by urging him to demand his rights as a husband, to reclaim his wife and children, by any means—the stronger, the better.

"And in health, for richer, for poorer . . ."

Geof had quit the force. Or tried to. But our chief of police had offered a more logical alternative, the one we hadn't considered because Geof had always turned it down before: a promotion out of the streets to an administrative position. It was long past time, the chief had chided him, it was appropriate, it was time for him to grow up into the authority for which he was suited and to leave the streets to the younger cops, the cowboys. For the first time, it appealed to Geof, certainly more than finding the bodies, than continually risking his life. He hadn't said yes, he had the length of our honeymoon to consider it, he didn't know if he could stand it behind a desk, if maybe he'd feel like a coward for doing it. But he'd still be a cop. That was what mattered to him, he'd still be a damned good cop.

"For as long as you both shall live?"

I glanced over Geof's shoulder to the family pew where my father sat with his wife, and where Sherry and Lars sat tightly together, his arm around her. There was a space between the two couples, and my mother occupied it, in my mind. My sister brought her husband's right hand to her lips and bowed her head over it. I looked back up at Geof.

"I do, too," I said.

About the Author

NANCY PICKARD IS THE AUTHOR OF *No Body, Generous Death,* and *Say No to Murder,* for which she won the first annual Anthony Award, given at the Bouchercon World Mystery Convention. A former reporter and editor, she lives in Kansas with her son and husband, who raises Hereford cattle in the Flint Hills.